ROAD TO REVELATION

A young woman's journey to faith and freedom

Stacey Spangler

This book is dedicated to *my Friends and Family.*

The whole lot of 'um.

Thanks for all the crazy adventures that have inspired so many stories...

PROLOGUE

'It really is like in the movies...' Gabby thought as she was hurled from the car, everything moving in slow-motion.

From the second she slammed on her brakes, which caused the car to lose control, time seemed to stand still and everything was magnified. Her seatbelt, which had been strapped across her chest (but apparently not fastened), had given way to the momentum of her body. The subsequent force pulled her to the left while it flung her through the driver-side window as the car flipped end-over-end. Gabby watched the jagged pieces of broken glass rip through her flesh as she was thrown through the shard-bordered hole where the driver-side window used to be. It felt like tiny knives skinning her bare arms and shredding her jeans.

Each individual sound was identifiable; brakes squealing, glass shattering, metal crunching, even her skin tearing. But unlike in the movies, where they say your life flashes before your eyes, what ran through Gabby's mind, as she was flying through the air, was a slow-playing highlight reel of her most memorable moments: seeing her parents smiling as she crossed the finish line at her track meet, playing basketball with her brothers, walking to school with Caroline, *the incident,* horseback riding with Jude, hugging her grandparents, running with her dog.

Then she had the briefest moment of clarity. One minute where all the months of inner dialog, the struggles of teenage turmoil, the layers of self-doubt, and the searching to find herself all became crystal clear. Years of questions and dilemmas rammed into milliseconds of revelation. The last sound Gabby registered was the 'smack' of her head landing on the gravel road. As she lay there unable to move, her eyes focused on the alternating lights of her car flipping. The bright floodlights on the front blurring into the red brake lights as it turned for the third and final time before landing inches away from her head. The cracked taillight, the one that had gotten her pulled over last week, was hardly noticeable now that the whole bumper was missing. She wondered, as the lights all faded to darkness, if her dad would still nag her to get that fixed...

CHAPTER 1

May 4, 2002

It is a quiet morning on the outskirts of the small, rural town of Ruthshire, Iowa. A cool, spring breeze blows through the trees and rustles the grass. A dog barks and a cow bellows a morning greeting. The full moon and twinkling stars give the pre-dawn hours an aura of calm while the looming sunrise sets a hazy tone for the new day. The normally peaceful town is even more subdued in these early morning hours. The atmosphere is nearly silent... except for the rhythmic thudding of shoes hitting the pavement.

Forty-four-year-old Donald Markson is setting a brisk pace on this chilly May morning. His 17-year-old daughter, Gabrielle, is matching him stride for stride. Father and daughter, running in unison against the darkness. Breathing in chorus. Neither one speaking. Gabby's three-year-old black lab, Missy, runs between them. Don sets the quick pace with long, easy strides. His years of service in the military, coupled with his tall, lean build, make running second nature to him and it is how he chooses to begin each day. For the past couple years Gabby has joined him on his 3-mile, early morning run.

Gabby isn't as tall or as lean as her father, but she is a determined runner who insists on keeping pace with her dad and, as a result, she does well on her high-school track team.

Don and Gabby share the same love of solitude, reflection, and exhaustion that running offers, it's one of the few things they have in common.

They jog past rows of houses in which most of the windows are still dark as the residents enjoy their last few minutes of sleep. They run to the edge of town where the concrete transitions to gravel and the thudding of pavement is replaced with the comforting sound of rocks grinding beneath their shoes. This signifies the halfway mark as they turn onto the gravel and begin to run back towards home along the cornfields that border the edge of town.

It's a tranquil scene... except for the palpable tension between the two runners.

There has never much talking on these early morning wake-up runs, but usually the silence is calming. The duo uses this time to clear their minds and prepare for the day. But today, the usually peaceful silence, sits heavily between them. Their relationship has been strained lately. Gabby is transitioning from Daddy's little girl into an outspoken, independent woman.

Don can see his little girl changing (not just growing up, but changing) and he doesn't know how to stop it. Yes, she is searching for autonomy, trying to find her own way, but he thinks she is going about it all wrong.

From Don's point of view, his teenage daughter is too big for her britches and needs to show respect. Gabby has gotten a wild hair lately; disobeying rules, rolling her eyes, talking back. The only way he can think to 'straighten her out' is to buckle down and be even more strict with her so she'll realize who is boss.

If you were to ask Gabby; their problems boil down to her dad being too over-protective and controlling. If he would give her some space to 'find herself' and prove that she's practically an adult and perfectly capable of making her own decisions, then she wouldn't have to be so rude.

Their attitudes towards each other are like flint and rock beating together, causing friction and igniting sparks. Don can see something is going on. He wants to help his daughter find her path. He wants to protect her from making the same mistakes he did and from experiencing the heartache he went through, but he feels like she's walling him off. So he pushes harder. And she pushes back. (Stubbornness was another one of the few traits she inherited from him.)

Gabby needs space. She is tired of people (mainly her dad) telling her that her hormones are causing her to be irrational. It's so much more than that.

Moodiness she could handle.

What she's struggling with, what is really bothering her lately, is that she literally feels like two different people. And she doesn't know which one she wants to be... or if she can even choose.

She feels like there's one Gabby; The Original, who is godly, independent, secure, sure of herself, confident, and... wholesome.

But lately there's a second Gabby; Gabby2.0, and she has equal pull. This Gabby wants to have fun, be accepted, she second guesses what other's think about her and she actually values their opinions above those who are closest to her. Gabby needs time and space to figure out which version she wants to be. She needs her dad to realize she is her own person. She needs to make the decision and she needs to do it alone. But instead of letting her become one of the versions of the Gabbys battling in her mind, Don is trying to revert her back into his little girl.

Now, in the breaking hours of daylight, Don and Gabby start to round the corner at the end of their road. In silent unison, father and daughter begin to sprint toward the wooden railing 300 yards ahead. It signifies their finish line. The first three miles of their run are done in sync, but this final stretch is always a race.

Gabby pumps her legs until they feel independent from her body. She concentrates on inhaling deeply, expanding her chest, loosening her arms, focusing on unclenching her fists and lightly pressing her thumb and pointer finger together like she is holding a potato chip. (A trick her track Coach, Mr. Johnson, instilled in the team.)

Gabby is mentally forcing all the energy in her body into propelling her legs faster and faster. She knows it's trivial, and probably stupid, but maybe if she could beat Don to the finish line, just this once, maybe it would open his eyes. Maybe it would prove to him that she is growing up. Maybe if she can show him that she's faster than he is, maybe it will help him to see her as an adult who is capable of making her own decisions rather than a child who he needs to protect.

The sweat from her brow burns as it drips into her eyes that are focused straight ahead. Her face, now damp from perspiration, feels chilled against the cool breeze. She's closing in on the target; fifteen, maybe twenty yards left.

Missy, also running at full speed, crosses the finish line and turns expectantly back towards her master.

Gabby tries to open her airways even further. She's breathing so deeply that if feels like her lungs are going to explode like overinflated balloons. She inhales through her nose, imagines the fresh oxygen flowing through her body giving new energy to her weary legs. Then she pushes all the air out through her mouth. She imagines the toxins she's cleansing from her system spewing into the cold wind as she exhales them. She completely empties her lungs before taking another deep breath and repeating the visualization.

This is it.

She pictures crossing the finish-line first.

Grinning ear to ear.

Then Don, coming in a few steps behind her, with a look of approval on his face. She pictures the two of them embracing like they would have a few years ago. The tension dissolved. Don patting her on the back and telling her how proud is, how he can see now that she's not being rebellious, she's just growing up. Saying that he's sorry he's been so tough on her, admitting she should have a one o'clock curfew....

Gabby can see it so clearly that her heart swells. Her eyes, already watering up from the cold, now begin to glisten with drops of emotion as well. She leans into the final few feet, exerting her last ounces of energy, just as Don sprints past and crosses the finish line, a few steps ahead of her.

Dang.

They walk home in silence.

As they pass her car in the driveway, Don points to the broken taillight and, still trying to catch his breath, huffs, "I thought you were getting that taken care of."

"Jude says he'll get it in whenever I take it down to the shop. I just haven't had time yet."

7

Don walks with both hands on his sides, still trying to even out his breathing, "You mean you haven't made the time yet. Gabrielle, you already had one warning, the next time it will be a ticket. I suggest you bump it up on your priority list." Don lectures her as he holds open the front door and enters their home.

It is always something....

Don heads up the stairs to get ready for his first job of the day; driving school bus. Gabby heads downstairs to her room to get ready for another day as a junior in high school. Missy follows right behind her, the dog's tail tucked between her legs as if she understands the defeat.

Another battle lost.

That brings the tally to roughly:
Don:1,987,655 and Gabby:0

CHAPTER 2

"C'mon, c'mon, c'mon!" Gabby shrugs her backpack onto her shoulder and yells up the stairs again. She has one foot propping the door open, the other blocking Missy from running out of it.

Seth, her 11-year-old brother, bounds down the stairs in two giant leaps, and races through the door screaming, "Shotgun!" on his way out.

DJ, her other brother, meanders behind him. Sluggishly yawning as he slips on a sweatshirt and grabs his backpack from the bottom step. At 14 he is in the throes of teenage boy hormones and hates, hates, hates, mornings. He sleeps until the last possible minute, and nearly causes Gabby to lose her mind every morning as he threatens to make them late for school. Every day.

The boys, (Gabby and the rest of the family affectionately refer to her brothers as 'the boys') couldn't be more different from each other, or Gabby for that matter, but the three have always been close.

Sometimes she gets annoyed with chauffeuring her brothers around, but most of the time they enjoy the morning commute. Even though it only takes about 10 minutes for Gabby to drive them to the middle school and drop them off, it's a little time for the three of them to catch up.

Plus, Gabby loves her car and any excuse to drive. She loves her 89 Beretta (an unhealthy amount really) maybe even more than she loves her brothers.

She revs the engine and they back out of the driveway. They are all excited about the weekend. Seth rambles on about going to Dusty's right after school today but DJ is quiet in the backseat. That's fairly common. He may be upright and moving but he won't actually wake up until around 10 a.m. Gabby turns her head slightly to talk to the hunched figure in the backseat, "I don't have practice today, you wanna ride home?"

"Nah." DJ makes an almost inaudible grunt from the backseat.

"You sure?" She probes, "It's not a problem."

Seth chimes in for his brother, "He's walking home with Lay-laaaaaa."

DJ shoots him a glare, but that's all the energy he's willing to exert. They drive down Main Street, passing the high school, to drop the boys off at the middle school which is another mile or so down the road.

When Gabby pulls to a stop at one of the only four stoplights in town, they see Jude, one of her best friends, walking from his truck to the auto mechanic shop where he works. All three wave and Jude smiles as he waves back and tips his hat. He's a few years older than Gabby but she has known him as long as she can remember, though it wasn't until a few years ago that they went from acquaintances to friends. Then one night, from friends to having (what Gabby would consider) a lifelong bond.

When Gabby had needed him, he was there and she knew he always would be. He won her respect, trust, and loyalty with one act... it was the only good thing to come from that night.

Gabby keeps her circle small, but the people in it really make her world go round. (She's actually said that line before and that sense of humor is one of the reasons her circle stays small.) Besides Jude, Caroline King is Gabby's only other constant confidant. The girls have been best friends since the Kings moved in behind the Marksons the summer before the girls started second grade. They were instant best friends. Initially because the closeness of their living situation, but it quickly grew into a deep friendship. The girls were very similar, and since neither had a sister to bond with, their connection deepened into more of a sisterhood than merely friends. Their bond is rooted in a similar sense of humor, need for independence, and a deep love for God.

The girls even look alike, but while Gabby's appearance is run-of-the-mill, Caroline is stunning... and an effortless stunning at that. Subtle variances make a drastic difference. Caroline is naturally model-thin, blessed with the coveted high cheek bones, clear porcelain skin that is contrasted by her dark brown (almost black) eyes, and a gorgeous mane of hair the same shade. Like Gabby, Caroline puts minimal effort into her appearance. But unlike Gabby, whose hair looks noticeably unkept, Caroline's has the illusion of hours' worth of work.

Arguably, the best part of Caroline's beauty is that she is oblivious to it.

Like Gabby, she puts her energy into areas other than getting dolled up. When the girls were younger, they would have sleepovers and stay up late into the night giggling about the goings on at school or their favorite TV shows.

Now, their overnight visits consist of in-depth talks about life, the overbearingness of their parents, and their futures.

Unlike most of the girls their age, their dreams don't revolve around finding Mr. Right. Neither girl is opposed to marriage, but their aspirations go beyond getting wed. Especially Caroline, who is a girl-power advocate if there ever was one. She is convinced she was born in the wrong decade. She has a 70's liberation soul stuck in a body that wasn't born until 1985.

Ironically, she is the one in a 'serious' relationship. Caroline, a very talented artist, has visions of moving to New York City and becoming a famous fashion designer. A lot of the time, while the girls are mulling over problems or dreaming about their futures, Caroline will do so while sketching an elegant ensemble into one of her many sketch pads. Gabby has her mind set on being a bovine veterinarian. Even with such differing areas of study, the girls still plan on going to the same college and being roommates. However, pastures full of the cows Gabby will attend to don't necessarily mesh with the runways where Caroline's designs will be displayed. But, the girls are convinced that distance won't be an issue. A bond like theirs can easily fare the test of distance.

And, obviously, they will both be extremely successful. They will have plenty of money to jet back and forth across the country to visit each other on a whim. The girls talk about their future often. In fact, the two talk about everything.

In her whole life, Gabby had only ever had two secrets from Caroline:

#1. The internal debate she wages with herself right now. Gabby isn't even sure what she's thinking, how can she express it to Caroline?

#2. *The incident.* But then again, she's never told anyone about that.

Seth continues to chatter until Gabby drops the boys off in front of the looming brick middle school. She waves goodbye and drives around the block to head back to the high school.

Today is a big day and she's anxious to get through it.

CHAPTER 3

Later that afternoon, Gabby is sitting next to Caroline in Biology class. Gabby stares blankly at the white board while Mr. Findel, their biology teacher, draws yet another arrow pointing at the hastily drawn squiggles (which were meant to resemble a frog) and continues to droll on about the intestinal workings of amphibians.

The classroom is a typical high-school science set-up. The stark off-white walls are riddled with cheesy motivational posters (like the kitten barely holding onto the branch with one paw and 'Hang in there' written underneath), diagrams, charts, and one standard-issue black clock, that Gabby is mentally willing to move faster.

The room is divided into two distinct areas. The backside of the class consists of three rows of long tables, all adorned with mini-lab stations that are complete with microscopes, test tubes, and paper towels. The front of the class has the individual desks clustered in a semi-circle, facing the ever-so-fancy whiteboard/chalkboard combo. Mr. Findel immensely enjoys flipping the large stand-alone contraption from the smeared, chalky blackboard to a crisp clean white board that he decorates with multi-colored markers, with just a snap of his wrist. He is the type of teacher who loves to teach and Gabby can't imagine him having any other occupation. He is great at what he does and he fits perfectly into the educator's mold. He's knowledgeable, has a dry sense of humor, and thick skin; all necessary qualities of a high school teacher.

Gabby leans forward on her desk, looking in the direction of the clock but not focusing on anything in particular. She's lost in thought as she subconsciously twirls her long, brown, slightly frizzy hair. She hasn't been introduced to a hair straightener (which would undoubtedly transform her wavy-ish mop of frizz into a smooth, sleek, flowing tresses like in one of those shampoo commercials) instead, she typically gathers it all up and secures it into regular ol' ponytail. Gabby is pretty. She's not stunning, but she's one of those girls who could be really pretty if she would, say, straighten her hair, wear makeup, or put any effort into her appearance. She likes the idea of being beautiful but she was not blessed with high-cheekbones, luxurious blond hair, or startling blue eyes. Her face is oval-shaped. Her hair is brown. Her eyes, well, at first glance they're an unremarkable brown. The flecks of green and gold that dance around are what make them entrancing, but that's only if you have the chance to study them.

No, she doesn't have stop-you-in-your-tracks beauty but she also doesn't have any off-putting features either. She is fortunate to not have acne or braces, and a few years ago, she graduated from glasses to contacts.

Unbeknownst to Gabby, her most attractive feature isn't actually part of her appearance. There is a quality about her that is magnetic to the few people she'll let see it. She has an energy that is so strong it can be almost repelling initially but then there is an intriguing pull under the surface. Her protective shell can come across as rude or standoffish but when you look in her eyes, there is a fire lingering beneath the surface that draws interest.

The class lets out a collective groan, breaking Gabby's daze. Mr. Findel's response "What? It's the truth!" lets her know that the groan was due to one of his many trademark one-liners. If she had to guess, she would say it was probably 'Repetition is the mother of all learning.' That is his favorite saying and he repeats it multiple times within each class period.

Without missing a beat, Mr. Findel dives right back into his spiel on the inner-workings of the amphibian digestive system and Gabby resumes her trance-like state.

She knows she should pay attention, but today is Friday and Friday's minutes tick past at half the speed of Monday-Thursday minutes. And this is the last class of the day so the seconds seem to span to hours. Still, she needs to focus. The highly anticipated dissection is happening on Monday. Most of the kids in the class are dreading it, a few make sick jokes, a couple claim they'll puke, and one girl, Hannah Naves, is boycotting it because, "It's cruelty to animals. All life is precious!" (*Eye-roll* Apparently 'all-life' stops at the doors of the high-school because Gabby knows that last summer Hannah's garage had an infestation of mice and Hannah had no qualms about her dad poisoning, beheading, or crushing every one of those little rodents.) Gabby is secretly excited about the assignment but she keeps that quiet because she doesn't want to be viewed as a blood-thirsty psychopath. She's not thrilled that a small mass of frogs will be sacrificed to let a group of high schoolers slice them open for a front row viewing of their anatomy, but she is fascinated by the way bodies function. After graduation next year, Gabby plans on going to college to become a veterinarian. That has been her dream ever since she can remember. Some kids flip-flop on their occupational aspirations. They start out wanting to be a fireman, a policeman, or an astronaut. Then maybe they switch gears to education (students tend to have an idealistic view of teaching, and who wouldn't want summers off?) Then maybe they toy around with being a doctor or a nurse before finally settling into a business degree.

But not Gabby.

Since the time she could barely toddle around, pulling on her German Shepherd, Tessa, while carrying around her calico cat, Critter, she has adored animals. As soon as she could speak, she said she wanted to be an 'animal doctor'. She would line up her stuffed animals and make her way through them using her pink plastic stethoscope and boxes of Sarah's real band-aids. Of course, her pets were always willing patients, too.

As Gabby grew, so did her love of animals. She eventually transitioned from 'playing' doctor with her stuffed animals, to finding actual patients who needed her. Over the years Gabby had rescued more animals than she could remember. There were the baby rabbits Gabby saved (and returned them to the wild) after DJ accidentally mowed over their mother. There was the injured squirrel she found on the side of the road and nursed back to health. (A story that had landed her in the local newspaper.) And, of course, the hamster epidemic of 2000 when the Markson home had unwillingly been the breeding ground for a small army of incestuous dwarf hamsters.

For the past 15 years Gabby has known that she wants to spend the rest of her life working with animals. While the occupation never wavered, her focus drifted a bit from the typical dog and cat doctor to a more specialized expertise... Bovine.

Gabby is obsessed with cows. Obsession may be too strong a word. Let's see, what would you call it when someone has their bedroom, locker, and car all decked out in the same black and white pattern, has voluntarily read multiple books on the anatomical make-up of said animal, and is studying to spend her entire adult life working with aforementioned animal? Intrigued with? Fascinated by? I'm gonna stick with obsessed.

Gabby is obsessed with cows.

One of the reasons it's so hard for Gabby to focus in Mr. Findel's Biology class (in addition to his bad jokes) is that she is part of an Advanced Placement program her school offers. Ruthshire High recently partnered with the community college in the neighboring town of Elesburg to have students take select college courses while still in high school.

So, four mornings a week, Gabby travels 20 minutes with five other students to attend the pre-selected courses. This semester is Animal Nutrition, Animal Science, and Agriculture Business. Right up her alley and Gabby loves it. She loves the content, she loves the challenge, and she even loves the commute.

"Uhmmhmmm." Caroline clears her throat. Gabby looks down on her desk and sees an origami triangle shoved under her notebook. She discreetly brings it down to her lap and unfolds it.

"Didn't we JUST talk about this???
How many times do we have to cover the SAME thing?
I know that repetition is the mother of all learning,
but seriously, repetition has got to be a great-grandma
by now.
Big plans tonight?"

Gabby stifles a laugh at the image of a word reproducing, but she quickly (and poorly) tries to cover it up by turning it into an obnoxious cough. This play on words is the type of humor the girls find hilarious but causes others to roll their eyes.

At the sound of Gabby's laugh/cough, Mr. Findel turns towards her with an accusing look on his face. Gabby tries to repeat the same pathetic laugh/cough sound to reiterate that it was real, while crumpling the note tightly in her hand. No need for him to investigate the passed note and call them out in front of the class... again.

The last time he took one of their notes and read it aloud to the class it had been a poem Gabby had penned about the absurdity of learning the reproductive patterns of plants.

It lost all comedic value when read by the person teaching the topic. Mr. Findel probably wouldn't be too upset about this note, but it's still best to conceal it.

After one more laugh/cough (that Gabby genius-ly finishes off by clearing her throat and making a production of patting her chest for good measure) Mr. Findel turns his attention back to the white-board and Gabby quietly flattens out the crumbled triangle on top of her notes about the alimentary canal. She grabs her pen to reply but hesitates with it poised over the paper.

Big plans tonight? That's a great question.

Gabby still wasn't sure.

The answer is complicated for a few reasons:

#1. This will be Gabby's first weekend off after her six-week grounding sentence. SIX WEEKS. She had been furious when her dad declared the punishment, but she hadn't fully understood how painfully long six weeks would actually be. It felt like a lifetime.

#2. With it being her fist night off, Gabby was really hoping to see Rick. She's known him for years (his parents are friends with Don and Sara) but they started 'talking' the day before her birthday (aka the night she broke curfew six weeks ago) so they have never been on an official date.

The initial conversation had gone like this:

Rick, "Happy Birthday."

Gabby, "Thanks, it's tomorrow."

Rick, "How old are you gonna be?"

Gabby, "Eighteen."

Rick, looked confused because he is eighteen and Gabby has always been a year younger than him, asked, "Really?"

Gabby, "Yeah, but not for another year."

There had been something endearing about her quippiness and sly smile that made him make it a point to talk to her again the next day. That initial spark was mutual and had grown. They started seeing each other during the break between classes and passing notes. (Like, old school passing notes since Gabby was grounded from her cell phone.) Last week when the final countdown to her freedom was in the single digits, Rick officially asked her on a date. Annoying as it had been, there was an element of fun to the creativity of the passing notes. But now, now they were actually going to go on a date and Gabby was nervous. She hasn't dated much. And to make matters worse, Rick is gorgeous. Crystal blue eyes, crew cut blond hair, and a charming knee-knocking smile that is perfectly centered between two dimples.

#3. And, of course, since tonight will be her first night of freedom, she works until ten. And Rick lives thirty minutes away. That will make it 10:30 before she gets to his house, and that'll give her one whole hour until she has to leave to make it home for her midnight curfew.

She REALLY wants to ask for an extension, but she knows that would be pushing it.

Caroline stabs her under the desk with a pen.

Gabby dazed off and now Mr. Findel is giving the final instructions for the lab on Monday. She re-crumbles the piece of paper and shoves it in her pocket just as the rest of the class is getting to their feet.

They all migrate towards the door where they wait for the final bell to release them.

Caroline leans against the wall and Gabby moves in beside her.

"Well?" Caroline raises her eyebrows and continues the question from the unanswered note.

"I dunno. I think I'm still going to go to Rick's. It'll just be a quick visit."

"You're going to drive an hour round-trip to be there for an hour?" Caroline made no attempt to hide the disgust in her voice.

"I'm still thinking about it." Gabby backtracks then quickly adds, "What are you doin?"

"I'm not sure either. Right now I'm heading to the art room to work for a while... we'll see what happens after that." Caroline shrugs noncommittally.

Gabby nods her head toward Russel, Caroline's boyfriend, who had been sitting next to them but was now talking to Nick Tanner, and she asks, "Are you guys doing something?"

"I think that's the plan but we'll see how the night goes."

The bell rings and Gabby follows Caroline out the door. Caroline looks back over her shoulder and says, "Well, whatever you decide, have fun, be safe, and don't do anything I wouldn't do." She finishes with a wink and a wave.

Gabby sighs. She knows Caroline is only kidding but her friend has no way of knowing how much Gabby wrestles with that exact thought.

Caroline has a strong, immovable moral compass. Gabby has a moral compass too, but her problem is that lately the needle has been pulling toward the south.

CHAPTER 4

Caroline exits Mr. Findel's classroom and continues straight down the hall into the oldest part of the building.

Ruthshire has grown sporadically over the years. What started out as a small farming community is now a full-fledged, idyllic mid-western town. The first industrial boost was the railroad. Next came the grain elevator. Followed by the factory.

With each influx of business, the population grew. As the town expanded, so did the high school. Originally built in the 1950's, it has additions from the 70's, 90's, and plans in progress for new construction to begin this upcoming summer.

With all the add-ons, rooms have been shuffled around multiple times but one that always remained the same is the art room.

Caroline made her way down the dark hallways and musty corridor before turning into her destination. The contrast was unbelievable. As soon as she opens the door, the dank, dark, hallway becomes illuminated from the light pouring out of the art room. The school was built on the side of a hill and though the surrounding hallways felt like crypts, this room is warm, bright and welcoming thanks to the floor-to-ceiling windows.

Caroline lets the sunlight wash over her.

This is her sanctuary.

She inhales the familiar scents of paper, paint, canvas and (her favorite) freshly sharpened pencils. She shuffs off her backpack next to 'her' station. There is already an easel and water dish set up next to a tall chair, tucked in a corner of the room.

She walks over to the long table that spans the length of the back wall. It is covered with a plethora of projects, all at various stages of completion.

Caroline studies some of them (paintings, pottery, sculptures) as she passes by to pick up her current project. She's placed hers in the back corner, it's easy to find. It's a large canvas, covered in mostly dark paint and the picture is still unidentifiable.

She carries it back to her station and begins setting up her supplies from her backpack, taking her time. She's not in a hurry, plus this is part of her process.

Slowly and methodically, she meticulously prepares her work area.

As she takes out each brush, blows on the bristles, and lays them in size order next to her, she can feel herself transforming. Her body is relaxing. The whirlwind of thoughts circling through her mind quiet and calm as she adjusts her easel towards the window to get just the right angle for lighting.

Finally, with everything in order and her canvas in front of her, Caroline shifts to the middle of her seat. She takes a deep cleansing breath, gathers her long black hair and, with a few fluid motions, sweeps it into a messy bun that sits on top of her head where it won't get in the way.

Now she can begin.

Her eyes focus on the canvas that is currently just smatterings of smeared paint, but Caroline has the completed scene in her mind. She sees both simultaneously and she begins to make the two become one. The assignment is to paint something that, as the art teacher Ms. Birdie had phrased it, 'soothes your soul'. On the uncompleted project table there were multiple beach scenes, a few majestic mountain ranges, and even a couple vases with fruit or flowers spilling out.

But Caroline is the only one who choose to paint New York City at nighttime. And it wasn't a peaceful view of the Manhattan Bridge reflecting the East River or a serene shot of the famous skyline. No. Instead, Caroline's painting would capture the essence of the city that never sleeps; Broadway after dark.

Billboards screaming advertisements for musicals and plays. Hundreds of taxi's waiting to escort the thousands of tired patrons home after a long night out. Yes, imagining this frenzied scene soothed her soul.

Oh, not the thought of being in the middle of all the hustle and bustle.

Thinking about having to elbow her way through crowds of people was enough to bring on a mild panic attack.

No, she chose this scene because this is the view she imagines having from her high-rise apartment. All the excitement, all the people, mean opportunities. She imagines her fashion designs being in demand for people both on and off the stages. She imagines designing the costumes for all the top-draws of the strip, as well as the high-end boutiques that line Fifth Avenue. Caroline has even worked on designing her own emblem. (But with the initials CK, there was already a very recognizable logo that she had to avoid resembling. She has a couple ideas completed, but she still likes to tweak them.) She also envisiones her nights in The City. When she isn't attending one of the leading plays (by invitation of the director themselves, of course) then she will be in her apartment, staring at this view, and painting for fun. Creating works of art that will easily sell for a hefty price tag.

That's why this chaotic scene is so tranquil to her. The lights, the traffic, the crowds, they all mean that she has finally arrived. That she is living her dream.

At least this is the scene in her mind. The canvas has yet to reflect any semblance of what the finished project will be.

Caroline has a system, her own way of morphing a blank canvas into a picture that seems to actually be moving. She has a gift that makes her paintings come to life. Gabby is her biggest fan and constantly in awe of her abilities. Caroline's talent is undeniable. Ms. Birdie thinks so, too.

Oh, Ms. Birdie... Caroline loves the eccentric (is there any other kind?) art teacher. Most of Ms. Birdie's students think she is a hoot. She is extremely talented and very... unique. She blew into town a few years ago and took over as the high-school art teacher, just as Gabby and Caroline's class moved in as freshman. She replaced Mr. Ricardo, the laid-back, slow-speaking, gruff, giant teddy bear of a teacher who retired after almost forty years.

Ms. Birdie could not have been more different from her predecessor. She is a short, round woman with pointy features that give her the resemblance of an overweight elf. She wears her hair short and spikey, and keeps it dyed a peculiar shade of red. The color is hard even for Caroline to identify (and she prides herself on her descriptive fluency with palettes). Mrs. Birdie's color is brighter than ruby but more muted than fire-engine red. It is darker than candy-apple but lighter than deep red. The color is, like Ms. Birdie herself, very unique.

Then there is the accent. Ms. Birdie has a thick Russian accent. No one knows (and no one asks) where she came from. It is more fun to speculate, especially with someone with such a colorful personality as Ms. Birdie. The most popular theory is that she is in a witness protection program, hiding from the Russian mob. Another rumor, on the other end of the spectrum, is that she is on the run from the FBI. Yes, these seem a little far-fetched, but the underlying question really is; without extenuating circumstances, why would anyone move *to* Ruthshire?

Whatever her past, now she is going on her third year as the Ruthshire High School art teacher and is doubling as the driver's education instructor. (Which is why Caroline has the luxury of working in solitude in the afternoons.)

Ms. Birdie offered to let her students come to her room before and after school to work on their projects because "One cannot put creativity on the clock."

Caroline is half-standing/half-leaning on her chair. She subconsciously nibbles on her lower lip and tilts her head from one side to the other as she works on angles, high-lights, and low-lights. She lets her hands create what her mind has already envisioned.

Her brain is blank except for the scene in her head.

Her whole body is focused on painting.

She is fully in the moment, entranced by her own work.

CHAPTER 5

Caroline had quickly exited Mr. Findel's classroom, seemingly unaffected by the tidal waves of students pouring out of the other classrooms and into the hallway. But the waves collide around Gabby, and she shrinks back into herself.

She clutches her books to her chest, readjusts her backpack, sets her eyes in front, and makes a beeline for the nearest exit.

Every time this cascade of high schoolers rush into the halls Gabby feels like she's in a scene from any typical teen movie.

She isn't the pretty, popular girl who leads around a small entourage, flipping her hair and turning heads.

And she isn't the classic nerd with the big glasses, lopsided braids, and braces who ends up out-shining Ms. Popular at the end of the movie.

Nope, Gabby is one of the un-named extras. One who, if they're lucky, will have their name scroll at the end of the credits just as the last of the audience is leaving the theater. It would read something like, 'Girl in Hallway - Gabrielle Markson.'

Gabby finally makes it through the sea of people and out the back door of the school.

She opens the door and steps onto the sidewalk that separates the large building from the small circle drive. This is the back of the school where there are only about twenty parking spots. These spots are coveted because they are close to the building, single stalls, and they make for an easier exit.

Fortunately, thanks to her college carpool that meets here at 7:15, Gabby and the rest of the AP crew usually nab one of the prized spots.

The warm sunshine hits her face and she closes her eyes. She takes a deep breath, enjoying the scent of the school's fresh cut grass mingling with the smells of fried food coming from Frank's diner just down the road.

She opens her eyes when she hears the door open behind her, but without looking to see who it is, Gabby starts moving towards her car to avoid possible small talk.

"Gabbs! Hold up..." Gabby stops just before stepping into the street and turns to face the familiar voice. Nick had dropped something, and when he stooped down to pick it up, the door had closed on his backpack. Like most of the kids in their class of 208 students, Gabby has known Nick Tanner since kindergarten. He is a curious guy. Tall and lanky with gapped teeth, a smattering of freckles and hair that is stick-straight but somehow always manages to look disheveled.

"Hey Nick." Gabby smiles warmly at him.

The anomaly of Nick is that in spite of his awkward appearance and general clumsiness, he is hilarious. His voice inflictions alone could take a regular sentence and put people, especially Gabby, in stitches.

He frees his bag from the door, walks over to her, and stammers, "Hey... I was gonna say.... I guess ask... maybe.... If you aren't busy.... Well, I have this comicon costume I'm working on. I'm deciding between Harley Quinn and Spiderman. Or maybe a combination of the two. I was wondering if you wanted to come over and check them out."

Typical Nick.

"Shoot, that sounds fun. But I have to work tonight." One benefit of working as much as she does is that it's always a ready excuse. 'Working' doesn't solicit as many questions as 'I have plans'.

She doesn't need to lie but she also doesn't need to mention the two-hour gap between quitting time and curfew.

"Yeah, no problem." Nick looks at the ground and kicks one foot aimlessly at nothing.

"I'll see ya Monday." She says with a smile. Then waves and turns to head back to her car. Nick watches her walk away.

Gabby has always been nice to him. He knows he is awkward. Most people either make fun of him or just ignore him all together, but Gabby has always tried to make him feel included. Like when they were in second grade and they were in the same class, seated at a round table with six other kids. Nick was terrible at coloring. He was terrible with coordination in general. But that particular day, they were coloring and Nick could not stay in the lines. It didn't matter if he moved the crayon fast or slow. He tried holding his hands various ways, nothing helped. His apple tree looked like the red apples were bleeding all over the green leaves. Brian (a decent colorer but a bully none-the-less) had noticed the scribbles and, as eight-year-olds will do, teased

Nick about it. Making comments about everyone else's picture looking perfect while Nick's looked like a kindergartners'. (A huge diss in their world.) Gabby had been sitting across the table from him, and while she was soft spoken and not one to be confrontational, he distinctly remembers her reaching to the middle of the table, grabbing a new crayon and scribbling over her paper. After she had ruined her perfect picture of two puppies playing in flowers, she looked up and smiled at him. His heart melted.

He has been madly in love with her ever since.

Gabby has always been kind. Not just to him, but to everyone. Even now, Gabby talks to him like a person while most of his peers treat him like an on-demand comedy show. Nick accepts partial blame for this because he found his knack for humor in middle school. There, he learned that he could offset his clumsiness and homely appearance by cracking jokes. He made it his mission to be funny. But even though it helped him avoid being made fun of, he still didn't have many friends. His peers don't really want to know him; they just expected him to entertain them. Now he isn't the target for ridicule like he had been in elementary school, but he isn't accepted either.

In eighth grade he worked up the nerve to ask Valerie, a girl in their grade, to the spring dance.

He didn't really like her but he knew she didn't have many friends, and she was also homely looking, so he thought he had a shot. In true Jr high fashion, he passed her a note during morning study hall. Valerie read it, looked at him, read it again, showed it to a girl sitting next to her, then both girls laughed. This time Gabby wasn't around but apparently someone had told her what happened (as is the case in small-town schools, even news that wasn't news travels fast) because when they were in algebra later that afternoon, Gabby brought it up in a nonchalant manner.

"Just so you know, Valerie is a jerk. Don't let her get to you."

"Get to me?" He replied with a mock dramatic tone, "Nah, it doesn't bother me. Humiliation fuels my self-loathing." He said with a grin and continued, "Good thing too, it was starting to run low but that should last me through the weekend. I can reflect on it while I sit at home alone, drowning my sorrows in Captain Crunch."

"Don't let Valerie make you miss the dance, you should go."

"While I do possess a certain set of phenomenal break-dancing skills, I think I'll get strange looks slow-dancing solo."

"Then you should go with me," Gabby offered. She said it in a way that didn't make him feel like it was out of pity or obligation. Gabby invited him to go with her 'group' which consisted of Caroline, Russel, Jude's sister Jamie, and her date. Nick declined at first, but after Gabby persisted, he agreed.

They all met at Caroline's house for pictures. Then Jude let them all pile in his pickup truck and he drove them the short distance to the school. Gabby, Caroline, and Jamie had taken the spots behind the cab of the truck so their hair was whipping their faces. Nick can still see Gabby's hair blowing in the wind and hear her laughing, that deep laugh that she hates but that changed his world.

When they got to the dance, most of the other girls went to the bathrooms for hair and makeup inspections. But not Gabby or Caroline.

Caroline ran her fingers through her long black hair and it settled perfectly into waterfalls around her face.

Gabby tried to run her fingers through her hair (which was as wide as it was long) but the natural curls twisted and became tangled. So instead, she bent over, shook it a couple times, straightened back up, shrugged her shoulders, and gave Nick an 'Oh well' smirk as she hoisted the tailgate closed.

He could tell she wasn't impressed with her wind-blown style but he thought it looked great. Then again, he always thought she looked great. It wasn't just her pretty face or athletic build, she is a good person. And she sees the best in him... she honestly looks for the best in everyone. He's not disillusioned enough to think Gabby is perfect. She's quiet. She can be reserved. She always seems to be weighing her options before she speaks. She is very guarded, but genuine. She chooses her words carefully, but always speaks the truth.

Now, as he watches her walking to her car, he's kicking himself about the Comicon comment. Just because he's a nerd doesn't mean he needs to lead with that every time.

Being weird just comes so naturally to him. He likes to think that it's endearing not creepy, but who can be sure?

He shoves his backpack over his shoulder and heads to Frank's to grab some fries and do some homework while he waits for his mom.

One of these days he'll have the nerve to tell her how he feels. He just hopes it's before it's too late.

In his mind, too late would be her finding a boyfriend or graduating and moving away before he has a chance to express his love for her.

33

He has no idea other events could steal his opportunity. Little does he know that tonight both of their lives will change forever.

CHAPTER 6

Don pulls the school bus to a stop in the designated area in front of the high-school. He's been driving the same route for 10 years; he has the hang of it.

He puts the bus in park and watches the groups of kids making their way from the giant brick school buildings to the waiting buses. He scans over the busy crosswalk and the crowded parking lot looking for Gabby, even though he knows she usually parks on the backside of the building where it's less congested.

The high school shares a parking lot with the elementary school that sits adjacent to it. Don watches the younger kids, backpacks as big as their bodies, scurrying to the bus lines. He remembers Gabby at that age, back when she was still his sweet little girl. Don's life completely changed when Gabby was born. His priorities, his ambitions, his career. Everything changed when Sara told him he was going to be a daddy. He retired from the military after eight years of service to take a position as a minister in their small hometown congregation. They packed up their exciting life in San Antonio, Texas and returned to the quiet simplicity of Ruthshire where they would be surrounded by family.

Don worked three, sometimes four, jobs since moving back. The only constant was his position as the full-time minister. His other jobs ranged from construction worker to bus driver and farm hand to dry-waller.

His days were long and full.

He begins before five a.m. with a bible study, then his morning run with Gabby.

By six he is driving his school bus route. Then for the rest of the day (aside from the two-hour block where he drives the returning bus route) he works other various jobs until nine or ten every night.

He has no downtime, and he prefers it that way. After all, idle hands are the devil's playground. Don never complains or brags about the hours he works. In his mind, it's just what you do. You work hard. You do what needs to be done to provide for your family. He has an old school work ethic... and he expects the same from his kids.

Gabby admires her dad. They have always been very close. He is her hero. He has always busted his butt to provide for the family. But that same grit that pushes him through those long days also blinds him to the joys of relaxation. He expects his kids to have the same determination and unrelenting schedule that he does. There simply is no time for fun. He doesn't see the point in days off, hobbies, games... or dating, for that matter.

This is the main disagreement he and Sara have. They rarely fight, but when they do, it is about the kids. Especially Gabby. Especially about his strict rules and high expectations for their only daughter.

He's not sure when or how Gabby grew up and stopped being his sweet little girl who looked at him like he hung the moon, but over the past few years the tension between them has been slowly festering and they are gradually drifting apart.

Things escalated last month after Gabby celebrated her seventeenth birthday and missed curfew. She had asked to go to dinner and a movie with a group of friends, and then 'out' (which Don knew meant they were going to be cruising central). 'Cruising' is a senseless pastime that most of the teenagers around town partake in every weekend, and sometimes even weeknights. It consists of driving up and down the main road in Ruthshire, turning around in the parking lots of the two gas stations located at the opposite ends of town, and then doing it again. And again. And again. He detests this activity. There are no redeemable qualities. It wastes gas, puts unnecessary wear and tear on the vehicles, and invites trouble. But, since it was her birthday, he had gone against his better judgment and consented.

Gabby had been thrilled. She huffed when he told her she still needed to obey her midnight curfew, but she agreed. When midnight came and went, he had gone to wait for her by the front door. When Gabrielle crept into the house at 12:15, he hadn't said a word. He just met her with an icy glare and a set jaw. Then he stuck out his hand, gesturing to confiscate her car keys. Gabby begrudgingly obliged by dropping them next to his feet. It took every fiber of his being to let that slide, but he did.

As Gabby turned to walk away, he knelt down to pick up her keys, cleared his throat, and stuck out his other hand, motioning for her cellphone.

This time Gabby objected. "Dad! I need my phone! It's my alarm and... what about if they need me at work? How are they supposed to get ahold of me if I don't have my phone?"

Still not saying a word, Don stood silently with his palm outstretched until Gabby slammed the phone into it.

Ignoring her hateful glare, he turned and went up the stairs while Gabby stormed down to her room. Now, you may be thinking that that was a fairly mild reaction for a teenage girl who had just gotten grounded from her car and gotten her phone taken away. And you would be right. But Gabby had been warned many times of the consequences of missing curfew. Even though she was angry about losing her car and her phone, she was prepared for it. The next day, Don had been making notes for his sermon when Gabby casually asked when she could expect her phone and keys to be returned, assuming it would be one week, maybe two.

When Don looked at her and stated very matter-of-factly, "Six weeks." well, that was when the fight exploded. That was when Gabby lost her temper and she waged into a full-out teenage meltdown.

"I AM SEVENTEEN YEARS OLD!!! I am the ONLY Junior in high school who has a midnight curfew! I work all the time and I am acing all my high-school AND college courses! What more do you want from me?!?!?!!?"

"Gabby, we are not having this conversation again. Case closed." Don's tone was even but firm.

"But DAD! You aren't even listening to ME!" With each word her voice raised a little and by the time she got to 'me', she was screaming.

Don set his jaw. His blue eyes burning holes through his daughter.

Gabby matched his gaze, her dark brown eyes brimming with tears of frustration.

"We're done here." And with that, he lowered his head and continued flipping through his bible.

Gabby screamed in exasperation, stormed down to her room, slammed the door, and blared her music. Don shook his head as P!NK's voice floated up through the vent. As he expected, a few minutes later, after overhearing the argument, his wife came in to pick up where their daughter left off.

Sara Markson had grown from the enchanting girl he fell in love with to a beautiful woman he still adored. She has flawless skin and long dark hair. To Sara's delight (and Gabby's annoyance) she is often mistaken for Gabby's sister instead of her mother. Now, Sara's brown eyes (a shade darker than Gabby's but with the same fire behind them) flared as she argued with her husband, making the same points her daughter had. Sara and Gabby perfected this unofficial tag-team tactic over the past few months, but Don was unwavering. The disagreement with his wife ended the same way it had with their daughter. But instead of blaring angry chic music after she stormed out, Sara seethed in silence and Don continued on with his study.

A six-week no-car, no-phone punishment would be enforced.

In hindsight, it had been a little harsh. His initial reaction was based out of fear from all the scenarios that ran through his mind when Gabby was late. But after he stated the punishment, he couldn't recant. He had to stand his ground.

He just hopes Gabby knows that he's so strict because he loves her. He is terrified she'll get hurt or make the same mistakes he did. The only way he knows to prevent that from happening is to hold on. To reign her in. To keep her close.

Maybe he should talk to Gabby about tonight.

He knows she wants to extend her curfew since she'll be working almost the whole night, but he also knows that nothing good happens after midnight.

Maybe he could explain to her why he won't relent. Maybe if she can see where he is coming from then maybe that will alleviate some of the hostility.

Aside from the initial outburst, she really had accepted the six week punishment well.

His thoughts are cut short as little Anabelle Grier, a sweet second grader who is a regular on his route, knocks on the smudged glass of the swinging bus door.

She smiles and waves at him.

Don shifts the lever to open the door to let the stream of kids load up. Annabelle is the first in line and gives him her usual, "Hi Mr. Markson," as she passes by.

She reminds him so much of Gabby at that age, with her long brown hair and joyful hazel eyes.

"Good afternoon, Annabelle." He replies and continues the greeting with every student who enters.

He knows each one by name and makes it a point to ensure they feel welcome and safe on his bus.

He is strict. Everyone is expected to sit on their rear and face the front. There's no nonsense or horsing around allowed, but the kids love him.

The next hour and half his focus will be on getting these kids home safely.

He'll think about how to address his own daughter later.

CHAPTER 7

Gabby turns from Nick and walks to her car.

Nick is a good friend. He's odd. Definitely a character, but he has a sweet disposition. If she didn't already have plans tonight she may have actually taken him up on the Comicon fashion show.

She feels bad for him, a lot of people don't give him a chance because he is... quirky.

She quickly crosses the parking lot and is grateful again that she doesn't have track practice this afternoon. She loves to run but she has a lot to think about today, and not a lot of time.

Luckily, practice was canceled because Coach Johnson is taking an elite group of runners to watch a college track meet and introduce them to the college coaches.

Gabby is not in the elite group.

She works hard but she isn't athletically inclined. She needs to get scholarships for academics, not sports. And once she is in college, her energy will be focused on devouring all the information she can, so she will be the best veterinarian possible. That excites and overwhelms her at the same time.

But all thoughts disappear from her mind as she slips the key in the door to unlock her car.

She smiles. Her heart swells with pride. She loves this car, her baby. She knows it's silly but she does, she loves it. She worked for, literally, years to be able to buy a car when she turned sixteen. She started saving for it when she was thirteen years old. She babysat, mowed yards, de-tasseled corn, babysat, walked beans, cleaned houses, babysat, shingled houses, cleaned the church building, and babysat. Every penny that didn't go to the church offering plate (Don's mandated 10% tithe) went into a car fund. She purchased her white 89' Beretta, with a red pinstripe, two months before her 16th birthday. Two months before she could even drive it. She spent hours cleaning it, sitting in it, listening to music, and enjoying the feeling of HER car. She would admire the dark blue interior, the dark blue console, even marvel at the simplicity of the dash. She took her time decorating it too. She had spent months picking out the right steering wheel cover (cow print), seat covers (cow print) and had chosen pictures of her with Caroline, Jude, and her family and tacked them above the front windshield. She had also covered up the unnecessary things on the dash, like the oil gauge and coolant levels, with a picture of Missy. One of her favorite touches is a stuffed cow named Bessie, a birthday gift from Jude, that stays buckled in the backseat.

Now, over a year later, her adoration for her car has only grown. She loves the feel of the engine, the seamlessness of the steering, the powerful bass of the tricked out sound system.

She tosses her backpack into the back and slides into the driver's seat. Her seat. Her happy place. She may be unsure of many things. She may feel inadequate at times. She may struggle with feeling torn between two personas. She may be searching for identity. But when she's here, in the driver's seat, that all melts away. She feels... comfortable.

This is one place where she is sure. She feels in control. She feels at peace.

Gabby leans back, closes her eyes, and takes a deep breath. Inhaling the smell of HER car. Just for a second, relishing again the... the freedom.

Then she puts the key in the ignition and her heart races as she fires up the powerful V6 engine. It never gets old.

She exhales and whispers, "I love you" to the car as she puts it in reverse, looks behind her, and backs out onto the street.

Gabby knows she needs to have a conversation with Don about her plans for the night, but he won't be home for a while. It's not even 3:30 and he will be driving his school bus route until about 4:30. They would normally both arrive about the same time, but with no practice, Gabby's afternoon has freed up.

So, with an hour to kill, Gabby decides to drive around and think of the best way to breach the conversation about extending her curfew. Gabby turns right out of the high-school parking lot onto Central and heads east out of town. Driving calms her. It helps her focus, helps her center.

She passes miles and miles of cornfields. The staple of Iowa.

Most people from out-of-state mistake Iowa for Idaho. "Oh, Iowa, the potato state, right?"

Nope. That's Idaho.

Here, in Iowa, they have corn. Lots and lots of corn. And Ruthshire is located smack-dab in the middle of the 'Corn Belt'. The town actually has an annual event called 'Sweet Corn Days'. Downtown gets blocked off, there's live music, a street carnival, and all the local vendors set up stands to give away, you guessed it, sweet corn.

One of Gabby's first jobs was detasseling corn. If you're not familiar with that terminology, in a nutshell, it's basically walking along the tall stalks of corn (in the sweltering heat of an Iowa summer) pulling the tassels off some stalks and placing little plastic bags on others. The whole process is done to protect 'breeding' of the corn. The last thing you want is a wild hybrid seed out there mixing with all your uptight, hearty crop. The job itself was terrible. It was hot. There were millions of bugs. Every inch of your body that wasn't covered in clothes became a battlefield of cuts and bug bites. The pay was so/so. The only real perk was the coworkers. Gabby got to work with Caroline. They carpooled in together and worked side by side all day. There were also the college guys who ventured back to town on summer break looking to make good money but still wanting to have their nights free to party. They were arrogant, obnoxious, annoying, and usually came to work hungover. But they were also good-looking and ripped. So much so that Gabby could see the muscles on their backs move through the sweat-drenched t-shirts. It made for a nice distraction instead of staring at the unending rows of corn. Gabby wasn't boy-crazy but she could appreciate a nice human specimen when she saw one. Simply admiring it, like artwork.

A beat-up red truck flies past her as Gabby turns off the highway onto a gravel road, making her way back to town.

By now she is ten miles out of Ruthshire, about halfway to Fairview.

That's the way a lot of small-town Iowa is set up. One small town fifteen minutes away from another small town, fifteen minutes away from another small town. The closest decent shopping area is an hour and half north in Mankato, Minnesota. Otherwise, Des Moines, Iowa is over three hours south. Sioux Falls, South Dakota is two hours west. And if you head east, you could drive all the way to Wisconsin before hitting any major cities. The Marksons don't shop much. Despite Don's numerous hours spent working, the family barely scrapes by most months. If they are lucky, they go shopping twice a year; back to school and Christmas.

Gabby smiles as she remembers one specific year her parents took them Christmas shopping in Sioux Falls.

At the time, they only had one vehicle, a beat up blue 1977 van. It was the type of van with bucket seats, dual opening back doors, and tinted windows. It always smelled like it had an oil and/or gas leak. Gabby had cleverly nicknamed it Ol'Blue. Don converted the standard-issued bucket seats in the back row into a shelf for when he was working. It doubled as a bed for the kids when they traveled. (This was back before seat belt laws were enforced.)

It was tradition in the Markson home to start and finish all the Christmas shopping on Christmas Eve. Sara swore up and down that they waited until the last minute because that's when they found the best deals. Gabby believed that was partly the case, but she also knew that her parents saved every penny they could so they waited until the last minute to shop so they could scrape together every possible dollar to spend on presents.

Gabby didn't mind the hurried, frantic pace that always came with waiting until the last minute. The hectic tone of the day was a tradition in itself.

The family would wake up well before the sun and leave early on the morning of the 24th, the kids sleeping through most of the drive. Then they would spend the day walking through stores in the mall while pointing out things they would like. Then Don would take the kids to wait in the car while Sara 'went to the bathroom'. She would quickly retrace their steps and pick up gifts to 'sneak' into the van. Even though the three kids watched as she shuffled bags into the back (rearranging Don's miscellaneous tools to cover up any hints to the contents of the bags) they all played along, pretending to be clueless.

The particular year flashing in Gabby's memory, the family had no more than gotten east of the Sioux Falls city limits, heading home, when the heat quit working in Ol'Blue. Don's entire body shivered as he drove. Sara sat in the passenger seat, shaking from head to toe, with her shirt pulled over her head into a makeshift hat, her knees pulled up to her chest, breathing into her hands. The kids curled up together on the wooden shelf/bed. Under a blanket, snuggled tightly, they sang Christmas carols. That year (like all the years before and every year since) the kids went right to bed when they got home but Sara and Don stayed up most of the night wrapping presents. Their funds usually didn't stretch as far as they would like, most years each child received only one gift so Sara often got creative with the wrapping. Sometimes that meant wrapping each animal of the Barbie veterinarian set individually. Or wrapping each piece of the spy set separately. Or even layering boxes inside of boxes and packing them with duct tape and bubble wrap to make the experience more memorable than the single pair of socks that were finally unveiled in the final box.

Gabby smiles.

Those were simpler times.

Gabby loves her family. She hates that her and Don have drifted apart. It's one of the many issues she is sorting out. She's wrestling with these two versions of herself, and she doesn't know where she falls. Much less how anyone else fits into the two-Gabby dimension. She doesn't understand herself... either of her-selves. She sees the distinct Gabbys, and no way combine them. How can she be strong, independent, and secure while at the same time being fun, carefree, and accepted?

As she thinks about this, two images pop into her mind; the cartoon version of each of these Gabby's. There's the 'Good Gabby' with big innocent eyes, holding her textbooks and a bible, wearing a wonder woman costume and a halo.

Then there's the new Gabby, the one who is unsure of herself and is just trying to fit it in... She's holding a beer in one hand (even though she can't stand the taste) and her cell-phone in the other, checking it for the text message she hopes is there, wearing a varsity letter-jacket and a mini-skirt.

She chuckles to herself as the wonder woman Gabby smacks the beer out of new Gabby's hand.

She continues letting them fight it out in her mind as she drives.

CHAPTER 8

Jude mindlessly taps the steering wheel to the beat of Sweet Home Alabama with Lynyrd Skynrd blasting through the speakers of his truck. He had taken a late lunch break and was now hurrying to make it back to the shop from his dad's house.

He sees Gabby stopped at the light and then watches her turn and head out of town. He waves but she doesn't see him. She looks focused.

He thinks about calling her (on her newly repossessed cell phone) but decides this is a conversation they should have face to face, and he doesn't really have the time to talk now. He's cutting it close as it is. An hour wasn't long enough for a trip to the farm to have lunch with his folks, but today he had needed to make it work. He had been so tired when he was leaving the field this morning that he took the old farm truck keys with him instead of leaving them in the ignition (where they had been for the past couple decades). The farm truck is a rust-covered, loud, rumbling Ford with holes in the floorboards and scraps of cloth barely covering the bench seat. But it is perfect for bumping around the farm where it gets covered in a fine layer of cow pies and corn dust.

When he arrived at work this morning and pulled out his keys to open the shop, Jude realized he had slipped the truck key in his pocket too. He called his dad, Roger, who assured him that it wasn't a problem; they'd manage without it for the day. Roger told Jude that he could return the keys tonight, but Jude had been looking for an excuse to visit anyway, he needed to bounce something off his dad. Planting season is crazy and there's not much time for chatting when they seem to always be going in opposite directions.

So, he volunteered to take his lunch break last, then he sped out to the farm where his step-mom had a nice hot meal waiting for him and his dad.

Jude comes from a broken home.

He hates that phrase because his family is one of the most supportive he's ever seen, albeit not conventional.

His parents divorced when he was a baby. His mom and dad had gotten caught up in a whirlwind romance as teenagers but are now great friends as adults.

People find it hard to believe, but Jude enjoys telling the story.

Roger (a third-generation farmer) had been immediately taken by the gorgeous Claire, who moved to town their senior year of high school. Her dad was a big-shot executive, brought in from Minneapolis, Minnesota on a 3-year contract to help streamline a struggling factory in Ruthshire. Her family moved to town in the January of '78. Claire and Roger graduated that May and were married in June. Jude was born the next summer.

Roger loved Ruthshire and he had no intention of ever leaving.

Claire was smitten with the handsome, rugged, farmer and quickly agreed that they could build a life together in the sleepy little town.

Unfortunately, she grew antsy. Even with a new baby and doting husband, she was restless.

When her dad's contract was up and he accepted a new position in a small town in Texas, not far from Austin, Claire wanted to go with them.

Roger couldn't (wouldn't) leave Iowa. It was a tough decision for them both. Claire loved her little boy, but she was only twenty years old. She had so much she wanted to see, so much life left to live.

Roger loved Claire, but his life and his family were in Ruthshire.

After hours of discussion, Roger and Claire came to an agreement. They separated amicably. Jude would stay with Roger but would visit Claire often, and she would return to Ruthshire to see him whenever she could.

Claire followed her parents to Texas, then Florida, before finally settling down in Colorado when she was in her thirties. It was there she met and married, Steve, a wealthy Internet whiz.

They would be celebrating their ten-year anniversary this year. Claire was now in her forties, and, by choice, Jude was her only child.

Roger had taken a different path. His heart was broken when Claire left, but on some level he had always known they wouldn't be forever. They were made from two different blueprints, cut from two different cloths. She had a sense of adventure and a heart for travel. He loved the repetitiveness of the small-town life and had a passion for farming. He thrived in the mundane; it would have killed Claire.

Roger felt very blessed that his parents were understanding of his circumstances. Even though they had warned the love-struck teenagers that the marriage wouldn't last, and divorce was very frowned upon in the tight-knit community, his mom and dad were there to help him when Claire left. They worshiped their grandson. Roger's mom was only in her fifties when Jude was born and she welcomed staying home with the baby so Roger could work on the family farm alongside his dad.

Roger was a devoted father to Jude, acting much older than his twenty years of age. His son was his priority.

After a long day of work, he still made time to take Jude to the park, to church, and to his doctor's appointments. That's where he met Sherry. Sherry had just graduated nursing school and moved to Ruthshire to be near her grandparents. When she walked into the exam room at Jude's one year checkup, there was an instant attraction between the bright-eyed nurse and the young father. Not the wild heat that Roger had felt with Claire, but a deep connection.

They started dating almost immediately. And, like with Claire, they were married a few months later. But this time it lasted. Shortly after celebrating Jude's second birthday, Roger and Sherry welcomed a second son, Joshua, to their family. A few years after that, Jamie made her debut. Just a few years after that, they were expecting again, another little boy. He would be named James... only James turned out to be a girl. They decided to stick with the name. Two years after baby girl James was born, Joy completed their family.

Stacey Spangler

Jude had a wonderful childhood, filled with great memories. Roger continued to be a picture-perfect father, taking Jude and his siblings hunting and fishing, teaching them the ways of the farm, and living the example of an upstanding citizen. Always there to offer advice, but also knowing when his kids needed him to just listen.

Sherry treated Jude as her own son. Lovingly tending to his needs and nurturing him into a caring young man.

Claire's husband, Steve, was supportive too, but since Jude was almost a teenager by the time he entered his life, his step-dad was more like a friend than a father-figure. And that worked out great because Claire was like a fun aunt. Always only a phone call away and always anxious for him to come visit. Even though they lived hours apart, Claire called every day and visited often. She also flew Jude out to visit at least a couple times a year.

He had the best of both worlds: a stable, loving family with a mom, dad, and siblings. They had big family Christmases and Sunday dinner each week. He also had the luxury of being an only child with his mom and Steve. (Though, they never missed sending a gift and birthday card to any of his siblings.)

He knows the arrangement is a rarity, and even as a young kid, he never took it for granted.

His dad is his best friend. He wanted to make the quick lunch trip today so he could ask his opinion about something that had come up. They had briefly talked about it, while enjoying the hot roast beef sandwiches and mashed potatoes with gravy that Sherry had whipped up, and Roger said exactly what Jude had expected.

He thought Jude should tell Gabby. Jude agreed... he just didn't know how.

Jude pulls into the shop parking lot. Throws the truck in park and heads inside. It's probably a good thing Gabby didn't notice him at the stoplight and that he decided not to call her. He needs a little while longer to figure out how he should phrase this. It's a delicate matter and he doesn't want to mess it up or hurt her. He'll think about it some more and swing by to see her at work tonight.

CHAPTER 9

Gabby is loudly singing along with Alanis Morisette, bemoaning the injustices of life, when she glances down at her speed; 70 in a 55. She quickly taps on the break to slow down, the last thing she needs is a ticket. She takes her speed down to a conservative 60 mph.

She's aimlessly driving around, lost in her own thoughts, and doesn't notice what road she's on until she passes Olson's farm.

As she drives past the large house with the sprawling yard her eyes are drawn to the long dirt path that winds through the cornfield to the clearing.

That's where it started. The scene flashes through her mind. One of the two most pivotal moments in her life that she wishes she could change. Gabby closes her eyes tightly and shakes her head, trying to clear the images. She opens them again quickly, forcing them back on the road.

Somehow she always ends up driving past here... one place she tries to avoid. But it's like a vacuum from her past, constantly pulling her back and messing with her mind.

Early last year, (when Gabby was only fifteen) the very popular senior, Hailey Olson, hosted a bonfire and Gabby was invited... in a roundabout way. Jude had been invited and he told Gabby she could tag along.

He was going to head out there around 9:30; but fifteen-year-old Gabby had a nine o'clock curfew. Not easily dissuaded, Gabby came up with a plan.

After spending the evening at Caroline's, Gabby made a production of being home at 8:30 and promptly saying 'goodnight' to everyone. She made it a point to say how exhausted she was and excused herself to go to bed at nine. At roughly 9:25 Gabby snuck out her bedroom window. It was almost too easy.

Especially since her bedroom was in the basement of the split-level home, meaning that it was exactly at ground level. It was the first of many times the teenager would use this unconventional method of exit, but she didn't think she had any other choice.

Jude picked her up at the pre-arranged spot at the end of the block. Ironically, where her and Don began their sprints towards home on their morning runs became the same spot Gabby would make her get-away while sneaking out at night, often by hopping into Jude's truck.

Jude is not just one of her best friends, he is very popular. He's not a jock. He's not rich. He's just a good guy who people can't help but like. He is tall, with dark hair and a matching beard that Gabby classifies as 'scruffy'. It is a slightly overgrown five o'clock shadow all the time. But his most defining feature is his eyes. Green eyes that shift color. Ranging from dark, forest green to a blazing emerald.

Gabby has known Jude for a long time. He is the oldest brother of her friend Jamie and, years ago, he adopted

Gabby as another little sister. They clicked right away and over the years have formed a unique bond. They are very close, strictly platonic. And while he was overprotective, he still let Gabby tag along on most of his outings.

So, that night, as Jude's truck rolled down the street with the headlights off, Gabby ran towards it.

Feeling anxious and excited, nervous and thrilled, with adrenaline coursing through her veins, she let the warm night air and the blackness surround her. Loving the quiet, appreciating the vastness. When Jude slowed to a stop, Gabby jumped in his truck and inhaled deeply. She loved the ever-present scent of worn leather, dirt, and... cornfield. From that point on, the night flashes through her mind like snapshots. Arriving at Olson's farm. Sitting on the tailgate with Jude, watching all the pretty girls dance around the fire.

Gabby distinctly remembers the faint rumblings of jealousy start to stir as she saw how confident they seemed to be, not to mention how coordinated.

Gabby didn't dance. Mainly because she couldn't. Rhythm was not in her repertoire. Jude teased her, gently slugging her arm and saying she should bust out her signature move 'the broken sprinkler'. She unwillingly patented the move last year after she attempted the 'timeless' (supposedly simple) move 'the sprinkler' in the privacy of her own home, with only a few friends present. She humiliated herself. She wasn't able to correctly time the hand movements with the slight leg turning. She had fallen and thus 'the broken sprinkler' was born. Of course, her friends still bring it up all the time.

Jude dropped the subject when she was adamant she didn't want any part of the dancing. She was perfectly content observing. People-watching.

When her cousin Miranda (Randy) came over, shot her a sideways grin with one raised eyebrow, nudged Gabby with her elbow and said, "The fire is gettin' a little outta hand, I think it could use a broken sprinkler." Randy was barely able to finish the sentence before she let out a soft giggle, with a wink and a smile... That was her signature move and Gabby knew (and had witnessed firsthand) that it made guys melt into obedient piles of goo, drooling over Randy, waiting to do her bidding. But it only caused Gabby to roll her eyes and Jude to let out a courtesy chuckle.

Gabby shot him a glare. Jude ignored her annoyance and allowed Randy to lead him into the mesh of swaying bodies.

Miranda Markson, aptly nicknamed, Randy, is two years older than Gabby.

She is the only daughter of Don's older brother, Dennis. But the family relation is the only thing the girls have in common.

Randy is a free spirit. Love and be loved. She especially wanted to be loved by Jude. Randy has big, curly, red hair and curves in all the right places. The cousins, though different in almost every way, get along very well. They balance each other out, complement one another. They don't necessarily spend a lot of time together, but there is an underlying bond between them. Some connection that can only be had when you're family. An understanding of past and persons.

Gabby rolled her eyes as her cousin shamelessly flirted with her friend. Jude had been a target for Randy since she was in junior high and he was a sophomore. Her pursuit was dually due to Jude's attractiveness and his dismissiveness towards her. Randy didn't come in contact with many men who she couldn't manipulate. If her always-exposed cleavage didn't do the trick, then her stormy blue eyes, full lips, and the laugh/wink almost always did.

Gabby turned away from the dancing couple. Well, Randy was dancing; Jude was more or less swaying in place. For as much as he teased Gabby, he really didn't have any moves either. Randy was a different story. Her body effortlessly kept pace with the music. All her limbs moving in unison. She appeared oblivious to the stares and completely unaffected by the attention. Gabby assumed she was used to it. Her cousin turned heads everywhere. Gabby didn't begrudge her that, what Gabby envied was Randy's confidence. Her security. The ease with which she handled herself.

To say Gabby was inexperienced in the 'boy' department was an understatement. Don was protective. Absolutely no dating until she was seventeen (a rule he stuck to) and if that wasn't enough, Jude was also against her or any of his sisters having any romantic interests in boys.

Gabby observed everything from her spot on the tailgate, taking it all in: The wind hustling the surrounding corn stalks. The stars twinkling across the vastness of the black sky.

She remembers being hypnotized by the roaring fire. The sense of awe she felt when she laid back in the bed of the truck, looking up at the stars.

Then being startled and flattered when Ken, a good-looking senior, sauntered up, leaned against the truck, and said, "Hey, you're the preacher's kid, right?"

Gabby felt her cheeks get warm. She racked her brain for something clever to say but, "Yep, that's me., is all that came out.

They had never officially met before.

She had seen Ken in passing... a friend-of-a-friend type acquaintance. Gabby was shocked when, after only chatting for a few minutes, he offered to drive her home. She wasn't necessarily ready to leave.

She was enjoying the loud music, the thumping of the bass, the warmth of the fire, the vastness of the black sky. But she also didn't want to miss out on... well, she didn't know exactly.

But she looked into Ken's eyes and they made the decision for her. She was a sucker for gorgeous eyes.

Gabby hopped off the tailgate of Jude's truck and scanned the dancing crowd for a glimpse of Jude or Randy. Her red-headed cousin was easy to spot. She was facing Gabby but had her full attention on Jude, whose back was to Gabby.

Gabby ducked her head and quickly followed Ken to his truck, glad to avoid Jude's definite opposition.

She knew he would object to her leaving with someone, especially a guy. She waited until Ken was driving through the narrow trail, his truck bumping over mounds of dirt, before she texted Jude to let him know she was fine, just a little tired so she was heading home. She slipped her phone in the front pocket of her sweatshirt and took a deep breath.

Ken's truck didn't have the pleasant, familiar odor she was used to in Jude's. Instead, it reeked of mint. When she saw the Mountain Dew bottle, half full of black liquid, a 'spitter' as the guys called it (an empty bottle they utilized to spit their chewing tobacco) she was able to pinpoint the smell... Skol. Gabby took a few deep breaths. Partly to digest the smell and partly to quiet her nerves.

Ken was carrying the conversation, if you would call it that, all on his own. Recapping his highlights from the last weeks' football game and rattling off the specs of his truck (engine model, dually, etc.) Gabby hadn't minded that he monopolized the conversation, she was so nervous she was only half-listening anyway. She had been concentrating on keeping her breathing steady, trying not to let her cheeks flush, and on keeping the quiver out of her voice for the one and two word responses she did manage.

She was trying to appear like anything except the nervous, novice, freshman she was.

Gabby had been so focused on trying to look cool, that she hadn't even noticed they weren't heading towards town. Her head finally cleared when they turned off the highway, and down a small farmer's road.

Ken stopped the truck and put it in park.

"What are we doin?" Gabby heard her own voice, which she had been working so hard to keep even, suddenly come out high and squeaky.

"Thought we could talk." But even as he said it, Ken slid to the middle of the bench seat.

"I really need to get home, my parents are expecting me."

"Thought you said you snuck out." Gabby's mind raced. Darn her and her big mouth.

Ken put his hand on her thigh. Her stomach dropped. The familiar blackness filled her belly.

The incident flooded her mind.

Her body began to shake and she jerked her leg away.

"I don't want anything to happen. Please stop. I wanna go home." She heard the words, but they sounded far off, like someone else was saying them.

Before she realized what was happening, Ken's mouth covered hers as he moved both hands around her back.

Gabby screamed and frantically searched for the door handle.

He forced himself on top of her, moving his hand inside her shirt. His calloused hands scratched against her smooth stomach before finding and cupping her bra. His other hand firmly squeezing her thigh, moving even further up her leg.

Internal lights and sirens went off throughout her whole body. Her hands were shaking. The black pit erupted in her belly.

Gabby gasped for air, suddenly she couldn't breathe.

She finally found the handle and pulled.

She toppled out of the truck and landed flat on her back.

Gabby looked up to see Ken lean out the passenger side and pull her door closed as he sneered and muttered, "Stupid freshman." Then he drove off, leaving her alone. After his headlights faded, Gabby was surrounded by pitch blackness.

The same darkness and endless skyline that had given her such a feeling of awe, wonderment, and freedom just a couple hours ago, now seemed to swallow her whole.

She gave her eyes a moment to adjust to the night and began feeling around beside her on the ground. Her phone had slipped out of her sweatshirt pocket but luckily had landed beside her. She picked it up and held it in front of her, steadying her voice and trying to think of what to say, but as the wind brushed through the stalks surrounding her, Gabby quickly hit speed dial four.

She will never forget the call, the one that solidified him as a permanent fixture in her life.

When she was cold and alone, enveloped in darkness, in the middle of a cornfield, he was the one she called.

Jude answered on the second ring. She could hear noise from the party in the background. "Hey.... Umm.... Could you come get me?"

"What? Hold on, I can hardly hear you."

She heard him say something, she assumed to Randy, and listened as the sound of the music faded.

"Gabby, what's wrong. Where are you?" Gabby looked around. She could see the highway less than a hundred yards away.

"I'm not exactly sure... I think a little past the radio station on HWY 4."

"I'll be there in ten minutes. Stay put."

She heard his truck door slamming as the phone disconnected. Gabby slipped the phone back into her sweatshirt pocket, shivered, and crossed her arms. She walked slowly toward the highway. Once she was there, she turned toward the blinking lights of the radio tower, still working on taking deep, calming breaths.

She felt dumb.

She felt used.

She felt alone.

She felt naive.

She hated every one of those feelings.

Was she overreacting? She hadn't been raped. She hadn't been hit. So why did she feel so violated?

Because.

Because of *the incident*, it made her hypersensitive to things like this.

Because she hadn't wanted it to happen.

Because that was her first real kiss. Ever. A first kiss is supposed to be special, an event, something that's supposed to make you giddy and daydream.

But instead, her memories of her first kiss would remind her of *this feeling*.

But damned if she was going to tell anyone what happened and have herself look like the idiot she was.

What was she thinking????

Getting into a car alone, with a guy she barely knew, without telling anyone?

So stupid.

She continued to mentally reprimand herself. Then she switched gears and began talking herself into 'getting over it'. She wasn't going to let this affect her. She had enough baggage from her past to deal with... this, this she would choose to dismiss.

She had been dumb.

Now she knew better. Lesson learned.

As she slowly trudged along the shoulder of the highway, she could see headlights off in the distance. Jude was heading her way, so Gabby began the quick process she had learned as a child to box up the feelings.

She couldn't identify all that she was feeling, but the hurt, the pain, the embarrassment, she imagined gathering all those up with her hands, packing them into a tight ball, and placing them in a box.

Then, she imagined taking the box, putting it in a cage, and securing it with a padlock.

Lastly, she imagined putting the box on a shelf. Next to all the other padlocked boxes.

This was a trick she had taught herself during *the incident*. When a young Gabby didn't know how to process emotions or identify what she was feeling, but she knew she didn't want to feel *that* anymore, so she put them away.

By the time Jude arrived a couple minutes later, Gabby had steeled herself against all the emotions.

She chose not to feel.

Gabby climbed up in Jude's truck. Welcoming the familiar smells of dirt, leather, and cornfield rather than Skol.

There was no lecture. There was no scolding.

He simply asked, "Wanna tell me what happened?"

Her answer matched his question in simplicity.

A monotone, "No" as she stared out the passenger window and felt the familiar void that always occurred after a boxing-up session.

"Okay, well let me know when you do."

They drove the rest of the way to her house in silence.

And that was that.

Jude never brought it up again.

And neither did Gabby.

She dealt with it. Or at least she thought she had. Little did she know that the stacks of boxes she had piled up weren't as secure as she liked to think.

Gabby convinced herself that once the emotion was locked away, it was forgotten.

But that wasn't the case. What actually happened is that she would have a moment like this, randomly driving around or sitting in class, and one of those boxes would fall and spill out. Then, after one box was open, it was a domino effect to others.

One emotion triggered another memory, another box. Her mind would be flooded, but still unable to process. Thoughts, feelings, and images would swirl around, but never find a place to land before Gabby composed herself enough to sort them all back into the boxes. Stacking them up again under the farce that she was in control. And, to make matters worse, Gabby built walls around the boxes to not let anyone in. She thought that building walls would protect her secrets, but she was also keeping people out. Never letting anyone help her sort through all the baggage.

Gabby shakes her head again, trying to clear the memory spurred by the dirt road from her mind, she turns the radio back up and presses her foot back down on the gas, imagining speeding away from the past.

Her denial of the feeling is one reason Gabby has been struggling so much lately with who she is.

She thought it was because of the typical teenage hormones (and that is part of it) but the more boxes she stacks without actually feeling, the deeper she buries her truest self.

She honestly doesn't know who she is. So much that forms her character is packed away and kept behind a lock and key that only Gabby possesses, but she refuses to use.

She has built strongholds around her heart and emotions. Gabby doesn't know who she is, so she tries projecting the different images of who she wants to be, the different images she thinks other people want to see. They are all shadows of who she is but none of them are the whole picture. Gabby is somewhat aware of what she is going through but she can't articulate it.

She seems stoic on the surface, but underneath is a turbulent mix of thoughts and emotions, swirling around at a thousand miles an hour.

Who the heck is she?

She wants to be strong.

She wants to be funny.

She wants to be pure.

She wants to be fun.

She wants to be liked.

She wants to not care.

Gabby wondered what it was like to just be... well, to just BE.

Ever since *the incident* she feels like she's been pretending, being someone she's not.

Her phone dings to alert her that she had a new text message.

She glances at it. Her mom is wondering where she is and saying that she needs to come home.

Gabby brushes the tears (that she hadn't even realized had formed) from her eyes and takes a couple deep breaths.

In milliseconds she envisioned all the open boxes being shut tightly back up and stacked neatly, orderly and put away.

This introspective stuff is for the birds. She doesn't have time for this. Right now she has to come up with a strategy on how she's going to approach the curfew conversation with Don.

She contemplates this as Destiny's Child comes on the radio. She glances down and notices, once again, she's cruising along at 70 instead of 55.

She slows down and remembers that she still hasn't gotten her taillight fixed.

CHAPTER 10

Meanwhile at Frank's, two overweight old guys are crammed into a table in the corner and signal the waitress back for the third time in twenty minutes.

"How can I help you?" she purrs, leaning over an empty chair, pushing her elbows together to further accentuate her already ample bosom.

"Ready for the check," the heavier of the two answers curtly.

"So soon?" She smiles a Cheshire cat grin, "You boys just got here."

The 'boys' had been plopped at that table since before noon and it was now after 3 o'clock.

"Gotta get back to the grind," Gus, the spokesman for the duo, an overweight sixty-somethin', with a mangy beard attempts to smile back at her.

He fails. Instead, his face contorts into a sneer, revealing a mouthful of rotting teeth. Without flinching, the waitress smiles, rips their ticket off her pad, and says, "Yes Sir." She uses an intentionally husky voice, holding each word out a beat longer than necessary. Then she seductively turns on one heel and walks back to the register, knowing that both men unashamedly kept their eyes on her the whole way.

She also knows that 'the grind' they need to get back to is actually just sitting behind the glass partition at the seedy hotel they own down the street. Gus is the sophisticated one of the pair. He mans the window while Joe takes care of all the upkeep and maintenance. By the overgrown lawn, broken windows, and rumored bed bug infestation, Randy would guess that he put about as much effort into the hotel's appearance and upkeep as he does his own. She has never personally visited their establishment, and couldn't name anyone who had... Actually, come to think of it, she never saw any cars there. Yet, Gus and Joe managed to come in here for lunch (and leave a hefty tip) every day.

Hence the flirtation from the waitress.

She learned a long time ago not to judge a customer on looks, especially in a bar. The dirtier and grimier, the more they like to throw their money around. She has been working here for five years and Gus' tips alone pay her rent each month. The diner-by-day/bar-by-night is a hole in the wall, cleverly named after the founder and current owner, Frank Halloway.

There are tables lining three of the walls with a long bar running the length of the furthest one. The formica tables are decorated with generic yellow and red vats containing off-brand ketchup and mustard, with a simple stack of napkins placed between them. The seats, barely a step above metal folding chairs, surround each table. Three TV's mounted behind the bar provide entertainment, featuring sports, news, and soap operas. All with subtitles running along the bottom.

There is a designated smoking section, but with the close proximity, the entire bar is always encompassed by a thin layer of hovering carcinogens.

Even with the dated decor, poor ventilation, and lack luster appearance, business is always steady. Thanks, in part, to the lack of competition in the little town but mostly due to the unique sites only offered here. Not scenic views. The windows face a parking lot and Central Avenue, the view that keeps people coming back is the waitress: Miranda Markson.

Randy had been waiting tables at Frank's since she was fifteen. It wasn't her dream job but it more-than paid the bills. If she wore a tight enough shirt and short enough shorts, she did very well. That was just one of the tricks she learned. She was the main draw of the bar. Frank knew it and compensated her accordingly.

There was only one Randy Markson, and she was nearing drinking age. She had a figure women worked a lifetime (and spent fortunes) to obtain and that men dreamed about.

Randy was 5'10, tall but not too tall. She has wild, curly red hair that contrasts her deep, stormy blue eyes and a chest that defies gravity; large but perky.

And, of course, there's the Randy Markson signature trademark; a smile and wink combo that turned men into puddles. Everything about her belonged in a Whitesnake video.

Today's ensemble is a simple black tank top that stretches so tightly across her chest that it looks see-through and rides up 6 inches higher than the design intended, revealing her flat stomach and belly button ring. She is wearing light-wash distressed jeans that look like they have been painted on, and she is rocking cowboy boots. She alternates between

Stacey Spangler

heels, converse, and the boots. There is just somethin' guys seem to like about the boots.

Randy graduated from Ruthshire high last year, but has no desire to leave the little town, or Frank's for that matter. She doesn't really have dreams or ambitions. She likes boys. Men, really. She developed a whole year earlier than any of the other girls in her grade and she remembers being the first one of her friends to get attention from boys. Especially boys older than her. And she likes it. She likes watching them try to avert their eyes from her cleavage or catching their sideways glances as she walks by in tight jeans that hug her luscious hind-end. She enjoys watching wives and girlfriends get mad. She likes watching groups of girls stare and snicker as she walks past, knowing that whatever cruel things they say are fueled by jealousy.

Surprisingly, Randy has no female friends.

She really doesn't have any friends at all.

She has admirers. Droves of them. She even has had a couple stalkers. But friends... not so much.

Men never make it past her body. She prefers it that way. She is actually very funny, in a sarcastic way, but her humor is usually saved for her own amusement.

Long ago, she had ambitions. As a little girl she wanted to be a nurse. Then, thanks to her grandma's love of Columbo, Matlock, and Murder She Wrote, Randy had dreamed of becoming a detective. But she has long since given up on any hopes past the Iowa border. She has resigned that this will be her forever home and her career will always equate to a meaningless job.

Her former ambitions and desires were barely a recognizable thought. It's hard to place the blame on any one person for her deserted dreams. It was a culmination of bad circumstances and bad choices.

Her dad, Dennis Markson (Don's brother) tried his best to be a good dad but he had continued to live the wild lifestyle the boys had enjoyed as young adults even after his daughter was born. Denny liked to frequent Frank's and the other small bar in town as well as any event that included alcohol. The brothers could not have raised their daughters more differently if they had tried. Randy's mom had split when Randy was only a toddler, she took off with a trucker passing through town. She hasn't been heard from since. Randy occasionally wonders if she settled down with that trucker and had a couple kids. Or maybe she was one of the Jane Doe's on the Forensic Files show.

It doesn't really matter to Randy, her mother is dead to her either way.

Like Roger's mom had been with Jude, Denny's mom had been happy to help with Randy. But, as Randy got older, more outspoken and less pliable, her grandmother had a hard time disciplining her.

Then, Dennis was laid off from his job working construction and, ironically, had to take up trucking. With her dad gone for weeks on end, Randy's behavior spiraled out of control. By the time she was thirteen she could pass for eighteen and she was doing whatever she pleased. Drinking, staying out all night, and skipping school.

When Dennis was home, he was too tired to implement any rules or boundaries. He let his daughter have free rein. He thought that by not arguing with her, and letting her have her own space, that she'd be more likely to confide in him and less likely to rebel. He was wrong. The more lax he

71

became, the more Randy acted out, leaving him feeling weak and Randy feeling unloved.

Denny started taking longer hauls with shorter breaks in between.

As a result of not being able to get her dad's attention, Randy tried to fill the void with other men. But she was never happy in a relationship and flitted from one guy to the next. Not intentionally, she was just discontent by nature.

She was always looking for more... for better... for different. Her longest relationship had barely lasted two weeks. She got marriage proposals on a monthly basis but couldn't imagine waking up to the same person more than two days in a row. Plus, there had been a few times when she actually started to feel something for someone, and that scared her more than the thought of being alone. Each time she started to feel like she needed someone, she would cut ties. If her parents taught her anything, it was that you can't depend on anyone.

But that didn't stop her from looking, experiencing, and testing out lots of options. At one time, a few years ago, she set her sights on Gabby's friend, Jude.

He was polite and courteous. They ran into each other on a few different occasions and she laid it on thick each time.

One night, at a bonfire, she had practically extended him an open invitation. She was dismayed when he turned her down. He hadn't even given an excuse. He had gotten a phone call and left, barely even saying goodbye.

She had been embarrassed. She liked to tease men. She found great satisfaction in being wanted. Embarrassment was not something she was accustomed to, and she really wasn't a fan of being told 'no' by anyone. She quickly channeled her frustrations into manipulation.

Instead of longing for Jude, she 'dated' his brother, Joshua, who had no qualms about loving Randy on the surface level, just the way she likes it.

Randy watches the overweight motel brothers heave themselves from their chairs and waddle to the door. She goes over to clear the table and is not disappointed with the tip. It's even a few dollars more than usual. Gotta love the boots.

Just as Randy finishes stacking the plethora of plates left on the table, the door opens and Nick Tanner sulks inside.

Randy's face lights up with a genuine smile. Nick is another regular who comes in three or four afternoons a week. He'll order a Coke and fries and do homework or watch TV while he waits for his mom to finish up work next door where she is a secretary at the courthouse. Since they share a car, she almost always drops him off at school in the morning, and in the afternoons he will either hang out here, or sometimes at the library, or take the bus home to an empty house.

Most days he chooses Frank's. The bottomless fries are a hot draw for the high-school crowd. And the waitress delivering them doesn't hurt either.

Nick is a good kid. Well... He is only three years younger than Randy, but he seems so innocent. It's probably the toothy grin, freckles, and the way his hair always stands straight up in the back, it reminds her of Alfalfa from Little Rascals. He (Nick, not Alfalfa) is adorable and Randy likes to have fun with him.

Yes, she teases him some, but his lack of attraction, and his docile nature, allow her to relax around him. He makes her laugh. And he doesn't drool over her like most of the customers. He is always polite and never makes inappropriate comments. She smiles and gives him a wave. Before heading to his table, she fills up one of their fancy red plastic cups with ice and coke, swings in the kitchen to drop in a basket of fries, and then heads over to see why he has such a long face.

CHAPTER 11

Gabby pulls into her driveway and puts the car in park but doesn't shut the engine off just yet.

She sits for a minute, staring at the house she's lived in her whole life. After pausing to collect her thoughts, making sure everything is locked up tight; Gabby grabs her bag and goes inside.

She is greeted by an excited Missy and the smell of fresh baked cookies. Her stomach immediately flip-flops at the scent.

Not out of hunger, but out of dread. Fresh baked chocolate chip cookies can only mean one thing in the Markson home; bad news.

Gabby's mind flashes back to the first time she remembers Sara ever baking cookies. She is sure her mom had baked cookies before, and probably even chocolate chip cookies, but none of them had been etched in her memory like one particular day.

It had been the middle of winter. A bitterly cold Iowa day. Gabby was twelve years old and in the sixth grade. Her love of animals had been nurtured for over a decade and Gabby had acquired a small zoo including; a cat, two guinea pigs, an aquarium, an iguana, and two dogs. Don and Sara consented to her collection with the contingency that she had to care for everything herself.

This particular morning Gabby rolled out of bed before dawn to walk her dogs. Tessa was a rambunctious, lively German Shepherd and Ruger was a happy, laid-back black lab. As was her routine, Gabby walked through the garage, let both dogs out of their kennels and headed across the street to the cornfields.

The Markson's house is set on the edge of town. To the south, rows of houses, but across the street, to the north, nothing but cornfields. Perfect for the dogs. Most mornings Gabby watched them play. Chasing each other. Burying their faces in the snow. Busting through the piles of fluff. But on this day, Gabby was humoring herself by making smoke rings with her breath in the cold air, when Ruger's deep howl snapped her attention. She jerked her head in the direction of the sound, just in time to see the back ends of both dogs running at full speed behind a bounding deer. Without thinking, Gabby started chasing the sprinting caravan of animals, screaming both dogs' names, but it was no use. They were gone.

Gabby slowed to a stop and fell to her knees. She started to cry, the tears crystallized on her cheeks. She stared hopefully into the horizon where the dogs had headed, praying out loud, "God please, please let them come home. Please God, please let them come home." After what felt like hours, with no sign of them, Gabby heaved herself to her feet and made the short walk home.

She vividly remembers walking into the warm house after being outside for so long. How her skin tingled when the warm air hit it. How she instantly started sweating, the sweat mixing with the tears.

Sara was at the top of the steps, helping 6-year-old Seth put on his backpack. Without turning around, she shouted, "Gabrielle! Where have you been? It's time to leave!"

The words choked in Gabby's throat as she cried, "Tessa..."*sob* "...Ruger..."*sob*"... ran...."*sob*"away..."

Sara ran down the steps and embraced her daughter, whose whole body was shaking. She assured her everything would be okay. The dogs would come home. Then she added, "They are just having a little Homeward Bound adventure of their own. Why should Chance, Shadow, and Sassy have all the fun?"

She was trying to make Gabby smile but was unsuccessful.

Instead, Sara drove the boys to school while Gabby changed and got ready. Then she came home to pick up Gabby, wrote her a note to excuse her tardiness, and took her to school.

That day had seemed to last forever. Gabby watched the clock, counting down the seconds until she could go home.

After the final bell rang, Gabby ran home. Literally, ran the whole mile between the school and her house. She raced into the garage and let out a sigh of relief when Ruger barked at her. She patted him on the head through the kennel and headed inside where she suspected Tessa was waiting for her. But she wasn't greeted by her faithful sidekick. Instead, she walked into the smell of freshly baked cookies. And Sara, telling her there had been an accident.

The dogs had been on their way home, right in front of the house, in fact, when a car took the corner too fast and didn't see them. The car caught Tessa's back legs with the hood. Sara had just gotten home from dropping Gabby off when she heard Tessa howl in pain.

Sara ran to her, the driver of the car stopped and also rushed to the German Shepherd's side. He called the vet, but Tessa died before Dr. Springer arrived. There was nothing they could do. She was gone.

Sara and Gabby spent that afternoon eating chocolate chip cookies and watching movies.

Two years later, on Christmas Day, Don and Sara surprised her with Missy. A hyper, wiggly black lab puppy that was now 3 years old. Tessa had been gone for 5 years. Ruger was old and gray but still a robust dog, just slower to get around.

Gabby's heart still hurt when she thought about Tessa. And her stomach still dropped when she smelled cookies.

It had inadvertently become a sort of sad tradition, when Sara had to deliver any bad news, she would make cookies to cushion the blow. A couple years ago, when Gabby's grandpa had a stroke, cookies before the news. Then when DJ's cat ran away, cookies.

Now... cookies. Why?

Gabby stoops down to nuzzle Missy's neck. The dog jumps into her, knocking her back into the door before licking Gabby's face. Gabby welcomes the affection with a laugh and scratches the dog lovingly behind the ears. Gabby gets back to her feet, bends over to kiss the top of Missy's head, and walks up the stairs. Missy follows but stops short of the kitchen and lays down on the top landing as she watches Gabby walk apprehensively into the kitchen.

Sara is pulling the tale-tell cookies from the oven.

Gabby's mind is racing with the possibilities of what could be wrong. Grandpa again? Grandma? Her brothers?

"Right on time." Sara smiles, but the smile doesn't make it to her eyes.

Gabby skips a greeting and immediately asks, "What's wrong?"

Sara looks at her daughter with a confused expression, then after a brief minute, realizes the baked goods have tipped Gabby off.

"Oh, nothing. No, it's fine. Everyone's ok." Sara gestures towards a shoe box lying by the top of the stairs. Gabby hadn't noticed it before but now she sees Missy watching it intently.

Sara looks at Gabby, shrugs her shoulders, and says, "Wafer." As an explanation.

"Ooohhhh." Relief floods over Gabby.

It was just Seth's hamster, Wafer. He finally died. Gabby feels sorry for her brother, but that hamster had outlived his lifespan at least twice over. Losing him was much better than any of the other scenarios racing through her mind.

Gabby, still near the top of the stairs, turns to head down to the basement. "I'm gonna get some homework done, any idea when dad will be home?"

"Any minute now, but Gabby..." Sara straightens up, brushes a stray strand of hair from her eyes, and turns her full attention to her daughter and waits for Gabby to face her. When she finally does, Sara finishes with, "Don't ask your dad to extend your curfew tonight. Be home by midnight."

Without a word Gabby's eyes narrow, she turns abruptly, and stomps downstairs with Missy at her heels. She storms into her room, slams the door, turns on her music, and throws herself on the bed.

She is so frustrated that she is shaking. She reaches under her pillow and pulls out her journal.

Yes, it's cliché, but Gabby keeps a journal, and has hidden it under her pillow since she could write. Putting her thoughts on paper helps her process them.

Gabby likes to think of herself as confident, self-assured, but the truth is, she is searching. She knows what she wants to be when she grows up... but at seventeen, Gabby is trying to figure out who she is now.

What helps, to some extent, is writing. Because even though she won't let her heart feel the emotions, her head can still process them.

Anger and frustration will bubble up, but before they can morph into hurt, her mind boxes them up. It's not the healthiest way to go through life, but it's the only way she knows.

So she writes. She writes her frustration about curfew, she writes about the dilemma with Rick. She even tries to write about the two Gabby struggle from the drive, but the words are even confused.

Gabby has a clear vision of the person she wants to be; strong, independent, tough, flippant with boys, secure. She works hard to cultivate these traits. That is WHO she wants to be. But as she matures and the walls are built higher, her sense of self is diminishing. The strong hold at her center is becoming more and more blocked off.

With that focus unreachable, she is inadvertently looking for affirmation in other areas.

She knows WHO she wants to be but the images and the shadows skew her focus.

When she nurtures her wholesome image: she grows secure in her faith and family, but she also grows bored.

When she nurtures the adventurous pull, the I-don't-need-anyone-image: then she becomes isolated. From her close friends and from God. She has a hard time finding the balance. She seems to swing like a pendulum back and forth. Going too far to one side then over-correcting. Never seeming to find that middle ground that will allow her to just be...

She knows that it is because she had evolved to the point of dictating her feelings instead of experiencing them. She has spent so long being removed from emotions that she isn't sure how to ease back in. She wants to be strong and stoic; but that leaves her unfeeling. She wants to feel deeply; but that will make her vulnerable.

Her words start to have a weight of despair to them so she switches back to writing about the anger from not feeling trusted, and the unfairness of her dad's strict rules.

She writes until her hand hurts. She lays down her head (which feels much lighter now with all her thoughts on paper) on her pillow and glances at the clock on her nightstand.

She still has an hour before she needs to go to work. She should get up and get ready but instead she closes her eyes.

She'll rest, just for minute...

CHAPTER 12

Gabby wakes with a start. She wipes the spittle from her cheek and grabs her phone. 6:20 p.m. Dang, she must've dozed off. Now she only has ten minutes until she's supposed to be at work.

No time to talk to her dad even if she wanted to.

She hurries to get ready. In one swoop Gabby slides out of her t-shirt while shimmying off her pants. She throws them both in her backpack, and quickly changes into a dress shirt and dress pants, the required dress code for the theater.

She grabs her bag and rushes out of the house. The obligatory, "I love you's" echo as she lets the door slam behind her. That is a non-negotiable in the Markson home: when you leave, you say I love you. Even when you're mad.

She slides into the driver's seat, turns the key, and lets the loud music and the thumping of the bass surround her, comfort her.

Meredith Brooks blasts from the speakers and Gabby grins.

Perfect.

She drives the short few miles to downtown, the heart of Ruthshire. She parks and steps out to admire the square.

Gabby has lived in this small town her whole life, she was born in the hospital that still sits proudly on the east of town, she was brought home to the same house they still live in, she is familiar with every square inch of this little town. Yet, she still feels a sense of awe when she is surrounded by these beautiful buildings that were already over a hundred years old when she was born.

This may be a sleepy old town, but it sure is pretty.

'The Square', as it is referred to, is a picturesque scene with the library positioned in the middle, commanding center stage. It is a grand building, raised in the middle of a lawn of lush green grass.

Flags will line the sidewalks on special occasions; Veterans Day, Memorial Day, and when a local serviceman or woman loses their life. That had been the case last year when a boy a few years older than her was killed while piloting a plane in Iraq.

The entire town felt a sense of loss. The sidewalks were lined for weeks with flags in his honor. Now a bench commemorating his life offered rest along the sidewalk leading to the library.

Across the street from the library is the trifecta of any small town main square setting: the courthouse, the police station, and the post office. And finally, kiddie-corner from those three stands the Grand Theater. It was one of the first theaters built around this area and no expense had been spared when it was constructed.

The movie theater is a staple of the quaint Square.

Next to the driver's seat of her car, this is her favorite place to be.

Gabby has been infatuated with it since Sara brought her see her first movie, The Little Mermaid, when she was a little girl. Gabby loves everything about this theater. The original old-fashioned marquee sign. The ornate decor. The ever-present smell of popcorn, which fills her nostrils now as she enters through the large glass double doors.

Immediately inside is the raised ticket booth where someone, usually her boss Rhonda, sits to gather admission with one lone computer. Walking past that, to the right is a large open area where patrons gather before and after the show to talk. There is limited seating, including a bench that spans along the entire front of the room (which is one giant window facing Central) and a single round table with four chairs pushed into a corner.

The concession area takes up the whole length of the back wall. It is blocked off from the lobby by glass cases that are filled with candy. On top of the candy cases are the cash registers, alternating with soda fountain machines. The wall behind it is covered in mirrors. The counters are filled with popcorn tubs, drink cups, the nacho warmer and the piece de resistance; the popcorn popper, sits smack dab in the center. This is Gabby's area. Her home, her space.

She works as a concessionist. (A fancy term for the people who dish out the popcorn and serve the other various snacks.)

Gabby hurries through the beautiful lobby. It's a large room, featuring an ornate looking carpet, and donned with velvet maroon curtains. Very classy. She ducks into the little nook of an office where her boss, Rhonda, is busy filling the cash registers. The technology they use is about as dated as the decor. The employees still have to manually write out timecards, use a calculator to balance the tills, and hand-count all the inventory. After a brief exchange of pleasantries, Gabby grabs two till drawers and takes them to the cash registers that are tucked in behind the concession stands towards the rear of the lobby.

They are the old-fashioned registers where the till drawers have to be placed in at the beginning of each night and removed after the last showing. Gabby walks behind the glass cases filled with candy, slides the drawers into the first two tills, then silences her phone and slides it under the third till that will remain unused for the evening. The third register is rarely ever used. It is reserved for blockbuster nights and big new releases. Like when the theater hosts the $1 matinees or when a new Star Wars movie opens. On most nights, the empty slot where the third cash drawer could slide underneath the register, made a perfect spot for the employees to discreetly hide their cell phones.

Gabby has never been the type to wait by the phone for a call, but she incessantly checks her cell lately, hoping for a call or text from Rick. They haven't even officially started dating yet, and so far he hasn't been the type to randomly check-in to say hi, but a part of her wishes he would. She wants to know he is thinking about her.

Gabby doesn't want to be the kind of girl who wants that, but part of her is. She doesn't want to want his attention, but part of her does. Yet another layer to the complexity that is Gabrielle Markson...

Gabby checks her phone one last time and feels her body sag with disappointment at the blank screen.

Then she tosses it back into the vacant cash drawer and silently scolds herself.

First of all: she doesn't know Rick well enough to let him influence her mood. This is ridiculous.

Secondly: She gets to work with Erik tonight, that alone should put her in a good mood.

Third of all: ... but her mental rebuking is cut short when the double doors swing open and Erik rushes inside. He pulls the door closed behind his lanky frame. His skinny-fit khakis and tight gray button-down are both wrinkled. He adjusts his large hemp necklace and runs his fingers through his thick-shoulder length dirty blond hair, obviously trying to compose himself.

Gabby assumed he was already here in the back. He was almost always early because, as the projectionist, he is in charge of getting all the movies cued up and ready to go. He would have to place the reels of film on the projecting machines, run through the priming strips, and have it ready for the patrons viewing pleasure in plenty of time to get the previews started before the actual show time. Gabby has never known him to be late and his anxious demeanor is also uncharacteristic. He is usually exceptionally (annoyingly) laid back. He generally radiates the reggae vibe.

A car horn honks just as Erik is taking his first steps towards the office. He spins around. This time Gabby notices his mom, Charla, waving a jacket out the driver's side window of her car.

Erik groans, darts back out the door and reemerges a few seconds later, carrying the jacket.

Gabby smirks and gives him a quizzical look as he hurries through the lobby, past the office, down the long hall that leads into each of the three theater rooms. Gabby is curious to find out the story that is behind Erik getting a ride to work.

Not only does he have his own car, he has a really nice car. The 2001, fresh-off-the-lot, only 15 miles on the odometer Jeep had been his 16th birthday present. He has proudly driven it all over the state of Iowa ever since, so the fact that Charla had shuttled him to work is both puzzling and hysterical.

The only reply Gabby got to her questioning look was, "It's a long story," which he muttered over his shoulder as he jogged past her to get the movies cued up.

They have been working together for almost two years but they've known each other since preschool. Long enough for Gabby to know not to push the transportation subject... yet.

She goes back to her business of unlocking the candy cases, filling the popcorn popper, and turning on the soda fountains. Gabby and Erik work together every Tuesday, Friday, and Sunday thanks to the set schedule Rhonda implemented last year which is mutually beneficial for everyone. The staff knows well in advance when they will be working, and it is a breeze for Rhonda to write the schedule each week. (Literally hand-write it with pen and paper. No fancy computer system for that either.) The team appreciates it, and when you factor in the other perks of the job (free popcorn, free pop, free movies), plus the fact that working at the theater is fun, the turnover rate is very low. Gabby and Eric were the last two people hired, and those spots only opened up because two of the previous staff had gotten married and moved off.

The theater employs a small crew compared to most places, and all in all, it is a great group. But Gabby is thankful that a majority of the time she works with Erik. He is Gabby's favorite coworker even though they are so different.

Gabby is a fairly conservative Christian, brought up in a strict household. Erik is a liberal atheist whose parents think that rules inhibit creativity.

One thing Gabby appreciates about him is, like Caroline, Erik knows who he is. He is the anti-Caroline.

Liberal, leftist, doesn't believe in a higher authority but thinks everyone has their own truth. Erik likes the grungy loud music and unknown bands. And if Gabby, or anyone else, recognizes one of 'his' bands or if, God-forbid, one of their songs is played on a local pop station, Erik immediately considers the whole band sell-outs, and he dives to the depths of scary punk rock to find another unknown he can idolize.

And of course, he sees nothing wrong with little marijuana (it's just an herb after all) and the government shouldn't be able to tell him what he can and can't put in his body.

These are a few of the various topics he and Gabby discuss during the hour or so when there aren't customers around. They have wildly different views on almost every subject; religion, politics, gun control, and the death penalty. But instead of causing animosity and tension between them, since they are both open minded to the other's opinions, they usually have lively discussions.

They also cover the general topics: which girl is currently fawning over Erik and which privilege of Gabby's is currently revoked. Gabby finds it ironic that in his quest to be so different, in his insistence on being so unique, Erik is actually stereotypical.

A popular rich kid who drives a nice car and is rebelling against 'The Man'. She is anxious to hear the story about how he ended up being driven to work by his mommy.

CHAPTER 13

Caroline adjusts in her seat. The art room is quiet except for the steady ticking of the clock on the wall and the occasional bird call outside.

She is concentrating, her head tilted to the left, biting her bottom lip, a few strands of hair have managed to loosen themselves from her bun and are framing her face as she delicately adds highlights and details to her New York scene.

She is in-tuned with the painting.

Focused.

She is suddenly jilted from her peaceful trance when Ms. Birdie crashes through the door, juggling books, an over-sized purse, and a stack of papers.

"Hello Dear!" Ms. Birdie greets as she clumsily waltzes into the room, making her way to her desk.

"Hey Ms. Birdie," Caroline straightens her back, rolls her neck, and looks at the clock for the first time. It's already past 6:30. She's been here for over three hours.

All at once she is hit with hunger pains, exhaustion, and the realization that she needs to pee. But she can't help but smile as the scatterbrained Ms. Birdie pats herself down, obviously looking for the glasses that are on top of her head.

Caroline clears her throat and sheepishly points to the top of her own head, cluing in the teacher to the whereabouts of her glasses.

"Oh, for crying out loud!" Ms. Birdie pulls the thick frames down to her nose and scurries over to look at Caroline's project as Caroline begins packing up her supplies.

"Breath-taking!" Ms. Birdie exclaims as she throws one hand over her heart and the other behind her back, leaning over into a bow, as part of the exclamation, but also to get a better look.

Caroline made a lot of progress today. The base of the painting had been done, so the details she added this afternoon completely transformed it.

"Thank you." Caroline beams. She loves creating art, but she also loves watching others react to her paintings. And Ms. Birdie never disappoints.

Ms. Birdie flutters back to her desk as Caroline finishes packing up her brushes. It's a much quicker process than the set-up, but Caroline is still particular, each brush has its own place.

When she's done, she takes her cell phone out of the front zipper of her backpack, turns the ringer back on, and glances at it as she hoists her bag over her shoulders. Five missed calls. Good grief. Two from her mom and three from Russell. She slips the phone to the back pocket of her jeans, says goodbye to Ms. Birdie, who is now frantically looking for her keys that are in her hand. Caroline shakes her head as she exits through the door. She walks down the short hallway and outside to the same door Gabby left through a couple hours earlier.

Caroline pauses to admire the sun sinking low in the sky, creating a beautiful color palette of pinks and oranges. The parking lot is almost deserted. The street in front of the school is quiet. She only has a short 1/2 mile walk home but she treasures the silence and solitude.

Unfortunately, it doesn't last long. Her phone rings. Loudly. She snatches it from her jeans and flips it open, seeing her mom's name on the screen she answers with, "Hi Mom."

"Hi sweetheart," Evelyn King's soothing, sing-song voice purrs in her ear. "I don't mean to bother you, I just wanted to let you know that your dad and I are going to be working late at the church tonight. I made you casserole for dinner, just bake at 350 degrees for 30 minutes."

"Ok, sounds good."

"There's also fresh bread if you want it."

"Thanks, Mom."

"And cookies for dessert."

"Awesome. How's it going at the church?" Caroline quickly changes the subject, if she didn't, her mother would go on all night. Taking care of Caroline is her mother's biggest source of joy, but she also loves working at their church. She and Caroline's dad, Mike, have been working late every night this week getting ready for their annual 'Friendship Sunday' that is happening this weekend.

"Oh, it's just wonderful. I am so excited to see everyone! I feel like we're really going to make a difference." Caroline can hear Evelyn smiling through the phone and Caroline knows her mom genuinely means it.

Evelyn King is warm, optimistic, and sees the absolute best in everyone.

Caroline didn't inherit these traits.

"How was your day, dear?"

"Good. I'm almost home."

"Oh Sweetie! It's almost dark! Where's Russell? I'm sure he would have given you a ride. Are you guys fighting?"

"It's fine mom, I'm fine, we're fine. I've gotta go. I'm going to make dinner and do my homework." Caroline isn't much of a talker anyway, but she really isn't a fan of phone conversations.

"Ok, I love you. Call if you need anything."

"I love you, too." Caroline walks in through the side door, turns on the oven as she passes by the kitchen on the way to her room.

The house is small but immaculate. Evelyn makes sure of that. Everything is in its place and the ever-present scent of cinnamon lingers in the air. The clarity she had a while ago is quickly becoming muddled as thoughts of her parents and Russell swirl around her head. Caroline is an only child and, obviously, her parents dote on her.

Mike and Evelyn King are still in love after almost 30 years of marriage and both relish the role of parent. Especially Evelyn. She is like June Cleaver, Martha Stewart, and Betty Crocker all rolled into one... with a side of 'Hallelujah'.

Caroline loves them and she appreciates them, but their love can be suffocating. She knows she's lucky to have parents so devoted to her happiness, but now that they're entering the final summer before graduation, she can feel her parents (especially her mom) spiraling to keep her close. They are terrified at the thought of her going to a big city. Mrs. King keeps dropping hints about all the great colleges and many opportunities within driving distance. Caroline loves her parents and she does hate the thought of leaving them, but she has a pull, a NEED, to GO. Her dream has always been to be an artist. She finds release in drawing, painting, and creating. She doesn't necessarily want to be a struggling artist, barely making rent, scraping together pennies for food.... Ok, yes she does. That's part of the journey. Paying your dues, scrounging for change, hawking your paintings on the freezing corners, using all the negative experiences to fuel more creativity. That has to be the beginning of the story if you want the rags to riches finish.

She wants to graduate college, then move to New York, get a job at a cliché coffee shop during the day and spend her nights painting. She wants to pour the anger, resentment, and despair from being a poor aspiring artist into her work, until she finally gets a break. A famous person, rich beyond measure, will see a piece of her art and have to have it. They will pay her thousands of dollars for one completed canvas. Then they'll show it to all their friends, who will then seek her out, she'll be in high demand within a month of being discovered.

Then she'll use that money to open her own clothing line. She'll bring her designs to life and they will be paraded down runways. She'll have her own fashion label, her own gallery, and she'll paint for fun.

But none of that will happen in I-O-W-A... no matter how much her mom wishes and prays for it. Gabby is fully supportive of Caroline's need to GO. Russell... not so much. He wants her to be happy but really wants her to be happy here.

Oh yeah, Russell. She should call him.

Caroline throws the casserole into the oven, sets the timer on the microwave for 30 minutes, and retreats to her room.

Unlike the rest of the house, her room is... unkept. Not messy, just cluttered. She has ideas and sketches pinned all over the walls. She has projects-in-progress, tucked in different places.

Mike built her floor to ceiling shelving that covers an entire wall to hold her knick-knacks, crafts, and paints. His hope was that it would help organize her room, but the massive structures only ended up giving Caroline more space to create and fill. Caroline pulls her hair from the messy bun, letting it cascade down her shoulders, and slips off her sweatshirt and jeans before pulling on a pair of Ruthshire High, size 2x, footballs sweats. She and Gabby found them at the local thrift store last year. They are absolutely huge on her, swallowing up her size 2 waist, even with the drawstring pulled as tight as they go, but Caroline loves them. Now that she's comfortable, wearing only her plain black t-shirt and the enormous sweats, Caroline grabs the sketch of the emerald green ball-gown she's been working on, her colored pencils, stretches across her bed, and calls Russell.

As the phone rings in her ear, she studies the face of the girl she's drawn to model this dress. She named her Emeralalda (like Ezmeralda, but a play on the color of the dress....) Gabby thought it was funny, too. They were the only ones. Emeraldalda has her hair pulled back tightly into a top knot, angular facial features, and narrow eyes. The dress is complete. It's a strapless, floor-length, emerald green color, with a back that rises above the shoulders, giving off a slight peacock feature.

Caroline is deciding which type of shoes this model would wear. She settles on emerald green high heels with fabric straps that will wind up the calf and be latched on the side, just below the knee, with a single diamond stud. She starts transferring the image in her mind to the paper in front of her when Russel answers on the third ring.

"Hello Beautiful." She has told him multiple times that she isn't a fan of that greeting. It focuses on her appearance rather than her inner character. Yes, she has positive outward features, but she would prefer that he recognize her talent, drive, or intelligence rather than physical attributes. But in spite of herself, it makes her smile.

"Hey, sorry I missed your calls. I got caught up in the art room."

"No problem, you home now?"

"Yep. Mom and dad are staying late at the church again and I'm finishing up Emeraldalda while I'm heating up the dinner mom made me... so I can eat it before the cookies she left for dessert... so that I'm hungry for the breakfast she's already thinking about preparing in the morning." She hears Russel chuckle on the other end of the line. They often joked about Evelyn force-feeding Caroline. It was funny for a few reasons. Mainly because Caroline eats like a linebacker but is built like a bean pole, and also because it is polar opposite to Russel's upbringing.

Russell is the youngest in his family. The only son with two older sisters. His mom has more a of 'let the kids raise themselves' mentality. Most of the time Russell has to figure out his own meals or join the Kings.

"I'm just finishing up helping my dad, I was wondering if you wanted to catch a movie or something."

Caroline frowns, looks down at her sweats, and looks back to her drawing. "Umm. I'm not really feeling it. I'm already in comfy clothes."

He doesn't say a word but Caroline knows exactly what he's doing. She pictures him, rolling his eyes, furrowing his brow, and turning his right palm up in the air in a "seriously?" gesture.

That's precisely what he had done. Caroline knows him well. They have been friends for a long time. They gradually morphed into a couple last summer. There wasn't a grandiose gesture or a decision to date, it just happened. They had been part of a large group of friends, then it was just Caroline, Gabby, Russell, and his friend Levi, and occasionally Jamie, who would get together. Then eventually, it was just the two of them.

Caroline loves Russell. Russell worships Caroline. So, his response to her declining a movie is, "Ok. What do you want to do?" Even though he knows she is already doing exactly what she wants to do for the rest of the evening.

"Well, I kinda want to finish this... I'm really close... I'm working on her shoes, so I just have the purse left." She could see Russell shaking his head.

"Ok, so maybe I'll see you tomorrow?" She can hear the disappointment in his voice.

They had talked about doing something tonight but Caroline generally prefers to stay home. Drawing, painting, reading, watching movies. She isn't big on crowds. Definitely never joined the party scene. The problem is, if her parents weren't home, then Russell can't join her for a night in. Those are her rules, not her parents'.

Caroline decided a long time ago that she was going to *wait* until after marriage. Russell was very understanding; more-so than a lot of other high school boys would be. It wasn't easy for either of them. Russell is extremely attractive. A little over 6 foot tall, with blond hair, and clear blue eyes. Not sky blue or baby blue, but almost translucent. However you want to describe them, they are hypnotizing. When he looks at her it feels like he can see her soul. It stirs feelings inside her that are scary, but exciting. That's one reason they have the rules.

Caroline knows it's hard for Russell too. But going against every teen-boy fiber of his being, he is supportive.

They work together to enforce Caroline's rules.

#1. No time alone in an empty house.

#2. No lingering in cars. (Absolutely no 'parking'.)

#3. No touching, other than hand-holding.

#4. No talking about anything suggestive.

#5. No kiss lasting longer than five seconds.

She had actually written them out after a church camp in 7th grade, long before she even had a boyfriend, but as the counselor said, that's the best time to do it.

Eliminate temptation instead of live with regret.

Caroline stuck to this resolve, for many reasons. First and foremost, it was hammered into her head for as long as she could remember that God created... *that*... for a man and a woman AFTER they are married. Secondly, she has heard too many teen-mom stories and she was NOT about to have her ambitions, hopes, dreams, and desires side-tracked by a baby. Thirdly, it would break her parents' hearts. She knows they don't agree with all her decisions, but she doesn't know if she could handle actually disappointing them.

Caroline knows it is hard for Russel, even though she was upfront with him before they ever became serious, she understands that he is still a guy. He tries hard not to get frustrated.

Russell isn't convicted, but he knows how important it is to Caroline to keep this promise to her parents, to God, and mostly, to herself. Her faith, her conscience, and her absolute resolve are a few of the things he adores about her. Caroline

Stacey Spangler

loves the phrase, "I am a true Princess because I am a daughter of The King."

But not a weak, damsel in distress, locked in a tower waiting to be rescued princess. No, Caroline sees herself as a warrior Princess. She doesn't wear her Christianity like a mask as some people.

To her, it's armor. When she feels weak or tempted, she knows she can step into that roll and feel strong, in control.

She's had her doubts but there is something deep down in her core that is unmoving. Her guiding light. Her faith. Her art. Her direction. This absolute resolve and sureness is something Gabby admires. And, at times, is jealous of.

Knowing that Russel is disappointed with her bailing on their plans, and making an effort to alleviate the disappointment, Caroline suggests, "How about we have breakfast here tomorrow with mom and dad, then if it warms up, we can go to the trails."

"Ok, I love you." She can tell he's pouting but he sounds appeased.

"I love you, too." She smiles as she hangs up the phone and settles in for a peaceful evening of seclusion.

CHAPTER 14

The night at the theater flew by quickly. Customers came, lines formed, Gabby was swamped. After Erik got all the movies rolling, he hopped behind the counter and helped out however he could. Filling drinks and buttering popcorn until the last of the customers were happily enjoying their film.

Now Gabby and Erik were seated at the small table in the corner, putting together the little cardboard kid-packs. The trays come flattened out in a box of 100. It was the concessionist's job to keep them stocked behind the counter, popping them up when the supply ran low. Tonight, it was running low and Gabby was happy to have an excuse to sit and listen to Erik regale her with the story of why Charla was his chauffeur.

"You lost your license?!?" Gabby couldn't keep the shock and mockery from her voice.

"I didn't loooossseee it.... It's suspended."

"What happened?"

"I was on my way to Spirit Lake, just passed the car shop and I passed a guy... and I got pulled over."

"You just passed him?"

"Yeah..."

"You got pulled over for passing someone?"

"Yeah."

Gabby gave him a quizzical look, "And that's why you lost your license?"

"Yeah. Well, he was turning left so I thought it would be safer to pass him on the right."

She pauses and thinks before replying, "But that road is only a two lane."

"Well, I opted to maximize the space and utilize the shoulder."

Gabby laughs. Her genuine laugh is deep and infectious. Even being upset and embarrassed with his predicament, Erik can't help but smile at her outburst.

"That makes more sense." She chuckles as she stacks the last of the trays. This violation, combined with Erik's two previous speeding tickets would be enough to warrant a suspension.

"I suppose this is just another elaborate plot by the evil government to hold down 'the man'?" Gabby continues to mock him.

"You're funny." He said in monotone voice, eluding that he did not, in fact, find that funny. Then, changing to a sing-song voice he says, "So, big night for you! Ungrounded at last... you going to Dick's tonight?"

Gabby knows this is his clever way of changing the subject. By undercutting her boy-interest, Gabby will correct him and that will become the new conversation. Even knowing his angle, Gabby can't resist.

"It's RICK. And yeah, I think so."

"So now that you can actually date him, what's the deal with you two? Is it serious?"

"Ugh, I dunno." By 16 years old, most of her friends had experienced heartbreak. Even Erik had been lovesick over Amanda Brown and was devastated when her family moved away. But he had moved on.

Over and over again.

Gabby has never fallen in love. It protected her from the pain of heartbreak, but she also feels like she's missing out. She casually dated a couple guys, but as soon as it started to get serious, Gabby would end it. When she started to find herself thinking about them when she was supposed to be concentrating, or when their face was the first thing that popped in her head in the morning, that's when she would break it off. Caroline theorized it is because Gabby is focused on her own life, her career, so she prioritizes herself instead of letting a guy dictate her actions.

Gabby likes to think that too. But she knows that isn't it, at least not all of it. She doesn't like to dwell on it, but if she had to guess, she would bet it stemmed back to *the incident*, and/or the night with Ken.

She knows that the incident changed how she processes things.

She knows she is more guarded than most. Protecting her heart and mind means keeping everyone at a safe distance.

She is friendly, but reserved.

Gabby gets up from the small table, leaving Erik to finish folding the last of the trays, and she heads behind the concession counter to make a fresh batch of popcorn. She's made hundreds so she can shift into autopilot. Pour in the oil, measure the seeds, flip the switch. Basic. But Erik continues heckling from the other side of the lobby.

"I like how you think walking away and acting busy will make me forget the question." His obnoxious voice rings out behind her as she stoops down to stir the popcorn already in the bin.

"If you must know... oh, I don't know." She says.

"That makes complete sense. I ask you how you feel about someone, and you don't know. Do you need to phone a friend? Bring in a consultant? It's not a hard question. Do you like the guy?"

"Yeah... obviously."

"Ok, do you want to have his babies?" Gabby glares at him in response to the ridiculous question but before she can come up with a clever retort, the front doors blow open.

Coming to her rescue, yet again, is Jude. He steps through the large lobby doors. He's dressed in his usual faded jeans and gives his customary head nod while pulling on the brim of his frayed hat.

"Just in time." Gabby smiles at him warmly while still managing to glare at Erik.

"Hey." Jude smiles back and moves towards the counter that she's still standing behind, by now the popcorn is overflowing the popper and spilling into the bin. Gabby listens for the cue (a 5 second popping interval) to dump the round canister into the open bin.

Jude moves closer to the counter but still raises his voice so she can hear over the popping, "I just finished up at the shop, thought you were gonna stop by to get that taillight fixed."

"Oh yeah... something came up." Her mind flashes back to the cookies, the hamster box, the scribbled journal entry, and the nap.

Sensing that Gabby wasn't wanting to go into more detail, Jude cuts in, "Well, I'm heading to Michael's for a bit before I get back into the field. Wanna meet out there when you get off to celebrate your reintroduction to freedom?"

"She can't. She's gotta hot date." Erik smirks as he answers for her.

Jude turns to face Gabby. "Oh, I didn't think movie night was gonna jive with your curfew."

"Yeah, we'll have to cut the movie short, I won't be there long, but at least it's a start." Gabby shrugs her shoulders and tries not to let her disappointment about the lack of an extension be too obvious.

The last of the popcorn kernels pop and Gabby hoists the silver canister over, dumping the fresh batch into the bin.

She continues, "Maybe we can do lunch tomorrow? I'll pick up Chinese and meet you in the field?"

"That'll work. I should be in the south forty about noon, just shoot me a text when you head out." With a wink and another tilt of his hat, he leaves.

He bought Gabby just enough time because as the front doors close behind Jude, the auditorium doors open, signaling that at least one of the movies is over.

Erik jumps up and runs to prop the doors open and reset the reels for the next showing.

Gabby stirs the fresh popcorn into the previous batch that was already in the bin. Then she wipes down the counters and prepares for the next set of showings which will bring the next wave of customers.

Now the countdown begins.

One more hour and she'll be done.

103

CHAPTER 15

Jude walks briskly through the theater parking lot, his hands are jammed into the pockets of his dirty jeans and his chin is tucked to his chest against the wind that is beginning to pick up. These early May days have beautiful weather but when the sun goes down, dang, it gets cold fast.

He makes it to his truck, opens the door and easily swings his long legs inside as he slides into the seat. He readjusts his used-to-be-black-but-has-faded-to-brown Iowa Hawkeye baseball cap and puts the truck in reverse.

He glances in the rear-view mirror and briefly catches a glimpse of himself as he backs out. His five o'clock shadow has officially grown into scruff. His usually short brown hair is peeking out the rim of the hat and starting to curl upwards, hugging the bottom. He makes a mental note to get a haircut, knowing that it'll be at least a month before he makes the time to actually do so.

He heads towards Michael's wondering if he should have talked to Gabby tonight. He didn't want to ruin her fun or come across as overprotective (she informed him that has been the case in the past) but he can't shake this feeling, the gnawing in his gut.

He has experienced it a few times before, always when Gabby or one of his sisters was about to get in to trouble.

The shrill ring of his cellphone interrupts his troublesome thoughts. He looks down to see the shop's number, most likely his boss, John Troug. Jude's mind flashes to an image of the overweight shop manager, pushed up against his always-cluttered desk. His big belly wedged beneath it as he taps a pen on top of it with one hand and, is no doubt 'smoking' an unlit cigarette with the other.

He has been 'quitting' for over a decade.

"Yello."

"Hey Jude, it's John. List'n, I'll get right to it. I hate to even ask, but Marshall is sup'pose ta open up the shop tomorra and he just called an' he's got a stomach bug somethin' fierce. I know tomorra's yer day off, but couldja run the shop fer a few hours in the mornin'? I got that danged funeral and I can't get here til noon."

Jude didn't have time to open the shop tomorrow. He's already logged over fifty-five hours this week at the shop alone (not including in the field) and he's been putting everything off, waiting for his one day off. But he knows John needs to be at the funeral. He had been working with John on Monday when John got the call that his wife's brother had lost his long battle with cancer (one of the reason's the cigarette remained unlit). While they had been expecting it, he knew the last thing John needed right now was to worry about getting the shop covered. And, it would give Gabby another chance to swing in a get that taillight squared away.

"Sure John, no problem. I'll be there."

"Don't know what I'd do without'cha. Yer a good kid, I 'preciate it."

"Don't mention it. Give Melanie my best and the rest of her family my condolences."

"Will do."

Both men hang up without any further salutations.

Ever since he graduated high school three years ago, Jude has been working as a mechanic at Ruthshire Tire and Auto. The Shop. He started as a go-fer while he attended night classes at the community college, but since he got his degree, nearly a year ago, he's been working as one of the full-time mechanics. With his years of experience at the front desk, and the gained trust of John, he also helps out in the office and has his own set of keys to the building. He loves his work. He loves solving problems, he gets along with all the guys, and the schedule isn't half bad.

The shop is his primary job but, like every self-respecting Iowa boy, he also works 'in the field' during planting and harvest seasons. He doesn't own any land (yet) but between his dad and granddad, he helps with almost 500 acres of corn and soybeans that need tending to twice a year. Right now, planting season is in full swing. Some people refer to the March-June season as spring, in Ruthshire (and a majority of small-town Iowa) it's referred to as planting season.

Like most farmers and their kids, Jude is in the fields a couple hours before heading to work in the morning, and long after dusk. He has never known any differently. Since he was barely tall enough to reach the pedals, he's been hauling corn, driving a tractor, and running to fetch things in the old farm truck. Before that, he was walking beans or tending to one of the other hundred jobs that need to be completed to make the farm wheel turn. It goes with the territory of living on a farm, everyone does their part. No exceptions. As the saying goes, 'It takes a village'.

There are times he despises living in a small town. The gossip, the rumor mills, the lack of privacy, but there are benefits, too. Like during harvest when everyone rallies together to get stuff done.

One example that he remembers fondly, occurred his senior year of high school. It was the first day of the school's spring break and his dad, who was only 38 years old, had a heart-attack. The doctors recommended a triple bypass, right before planting began. Sherry was distraught and refused to leave his side. She stayed with him in the hospital night and day. Roger worried about the farm, it didn't matter how much everyone assured him they would get it figured out, Roger still worried. He insisted Jude stay on the farm and skip school the last two months of his senior year, even though that meant he may not graduate. The farm was their only source of income. The livelihood of the family depended on a successful crop.

As much as Jude wanted to stay with his dad, he knew he was needed on the farm and he respected Roger's wishes. He spent the whole next week preparing for planting. Making sure everything was in order. The following week, the first Monday Jude would have missed school, Jude and his granddad came over early in the morning to take care of their small herd of cattle. When they topped the hill overlooking their land, they were amazed to see dozens of planters in various parts of the field. Friends and neighbors were all working together to get the seeds in the ground.

Jude had never seen his granddad show much emotion, but when he glanced over that morning, his mountain of a grandfather had tears shimmering in his eyes. One of their neighbors was already watering the cattle trough, when they pulled in, he explained that they had it all figured out. Everyone was taking shifts the next two months to make sure Roger's fields were taken care if. Roger had always been there for anyone in need, it was the least they could do. They were happy to help. Jude would still need to work the fields, but he would go to school as usual.

They ended up with a bumper crop that year.

Not only that, but Sherry didn't have to worry about feeding their family at all. Every afternoon a fully prepared meal showed up on the front porch. Jude and his family will never know how many people chipped in to help take care of their family during those trying couple months, but their gratitude was immeasurable.

There were more examples of the town rallying together, but this was Jude's favorite. Everyone did their part. The farming community was a good group of folks. And even people who lived in town were happy to lend a hand. Like Gabby. She always helped out. Before she could drive, she would ask Sara to bring her out with snacks and coffee.

Jude loves Gabby. He does. It is something he takes a lot of grief for; a 21-year-old guy hanging out platonic-ally with a good-looking 17-year-old girl... he knows they are the topics of rumors circulating around town. And for those who are close them, who know they are merely friends and not love-interests, well, they are the worst. Especially Jude's younger brother and his group of friends. Gabby obviously loves Jude, too and people can't understand why nothing has happened between them.

Gabby is pretty. Jude knows she feels out-shined by Caroline (who is stunningly beautiful, there is no denying that) but Gabby has an endearing quality about her. And she has an energy that seems always just below the surface. Whether it is her drive for success or her sheer willpower, something about Gabby is electric.

And yet, they are just friends.

He has known her almost her whole life, but up until a few years ago, she had been less of a friend, and more like another annoying little sister, joining the three biological ones he already has.

His family lives down the road from Caroline King's family and his sister Jamie is in the same grade as the girls. The small pack had been hanging around his house, and invading his space, since they were barely able to ride their bikes down the street. Even when the girls matured into junior high, he still saw them as 6-year-olds, with pig tails, playing dress-up and swinging on the tire swing. The shift from annoying little sister to close friend happened when Jude was a senior and the girls were in their 8th grade year.

Jude found out that some of the idiot high-school boys, including his brother, had created a game of conquests. There was a point system based on age, looks, and assumed attainability and point values assigned for various acts. Sisters of any of the participants were off-limits, but that was it. Targets included most of the high-school girls, a few of the incoming freshman (who were only 14 at the time) and even a few of the younger teachers. Besides the teachers, Gabby Markson and Caroline King were a couple of the highest point values on the list. Caroline because of her bible-toting, scripture-quoting personality, and her general disdain for the male gender (but with them generating activities like this one, Jude thought her disdain was justified) and Gabby because she was also a goody-two shoes AND a preacher's kid.

After Jude yelled at his brother, trying to explain to his hormone-impaired brain why this was so degrading, doing his best to show him how horrible the game was, and wondering where he had gone wrong as an older brother, he went on a rampage to deal with all the other testosterone driven imbeciles. He made the rounds to all the groups of congregated over-grown, pubescent, toddlers with facial hair and gave them the same lecture he'd given his brother. Telling them how degrading, not to mention illegal, their little game was and how he thought it should come to an immediate stop but if they insisted on continuing, Gabby and Caroline were strictly off-limits. After sufficiently threatening all the boys involved and, spreading the word around to anyone who would listen, he assumed the matter was over with.

Then, on a rainy afternoon, later the next week, he picked up Jamie, Caroline, and Gabby to give them a dry ride home.

They all squeezed into the cab of his truck and Jamie immediately began teasing Gabby. After not much probing, his little sister blurted out that Trevor (a good-looking albeit chubby sophomore) had asked Gabby 'out' on Friday night.

Jude could tell Gabby was embarrassed and she became defensive. Her dad would never let her date anyway...

Jude knew Trevor. He'd known him whole life. There was no way he had pure intentions for asking an 8th grader on a date, but he had an idea. He told Gabby to say yes. He told Gabby to tell her folks that she was staying the night with Jamie on Friday. She would come to their house after school and meet Trevor at the Casey's gas station at seven.

Gabby did as Jude told her. Don and Sara were used to her staying at Caroline's or Jamie's house, so they didn't think anything of it. After school the girls went to Jamie's and watched a couple episodes of Saved by the Bell while they worked together to get Gabby 'ready'. Jamie applied thick blue eyeshadow (that Gabby wiped off) and Caroline braided her hair (which Gabby took out). At 7:00 she was waiting outside the front door of Casey's when Trevor pulled up in his Toyota Camry. Gabby walked over and slid into the passenger seat and, as planned, Jude walked from the side of the building and climbed in the backseat.

He'll never forget the look on Trevor's face when the pieces clicked. The three of them had a lovely date. Trevor treated them all to dinner and a movie, where Jude sat between them. That was the first time he had spent time with Gabby apart from her entourage.

Over the next few months, they spent more and more time without the other girls. Gabby wasn't giggly and shallow like most of Jamie's friends. She was mature, smart, and funny. He enjoyed spending time with her. And there was something else... in addition to her drive and passion, there is something else lurking below the surface that, even after all this time, he can't put his finger on.

He has never told her the real reason he had joined them on their date. She still thinks he was just chaperoning. He didn't think the girls needed to know the ugly truth about how vile boys can be, at least not yet.

And Gabby had no idea that after Trevor dropped them back off at Casey's and Jude drove her back to his house, he had driven to Trevor's house and had a nice chat with him and his brother. Trevor's brother, Corey, was a good friend of

Jude and was equally as appalled to learn about the point system. Jude knew Corey would deal with it. And he had.

Gabby knew nothing about it. Just like she didn't know that he asked around after Hayley Olson's bonfire and found out that Ken was the one who deserted her on the side of the road. After more investigating, Jude learned the whole story, and he dealt with Ken himself.

It took a lot to make Jude angry, but when it happened, he was a force to be reckoned with.

Now he was getting that stirring again, the weird feeling in his gut that he'd had when the girls told him about the date with Trevor. The one he had when he noticed Gabby had left the bonfire without him.

He has never been a fan of this Rick guy, but Gabby is long past the age of letting him tag along on dates.

Then, yesterday, he overheard one of the guys who frequents the shop (but never brings anything in for repair, it's just a social event for him) say that his niece, who lives twenty minutes the opposite way, was back with some boy from Elesburg.

Jude isn't positive but he has a strong suspicion (based on the description of the truck and the references to the family) that it is Rick. Ya gotta love small towns.

Jude thought he should tell Gabby, but he didn't want to stick his nose where it didn't belong. That's why he wanted to ask Roger's opinion first. And Roger concurred.

Better to chance Jude hurting Gabby's feelings than to risk her falling for this guy and having him crush her.

Tonight he'd suck it up and let her enjoy herself.

Tomorrow he'd tell her. Tomorrow.

She'll be fine for one night.

CHAPTER 16

Gabby finishes wiping down the last counter, grabs her phone from under the cash register, and slides it in her pocket. She quickly walks to the office and pulls out her timecard.

"That was quick," Rhonda comments as she pauses from counting the cash in the till and spins around to face Gabby. Gabby sped through the closing routine and is leaving 10 minutes earlier than usual.

"Gotta hot date?" Rhonda asks with a smirk. Gabby can't tell if she overheard the conversation with Erik or if she's just giving Gabby a hard time.

Gabby assumes the latter and replies with, "It's freezing cold outside, I'd be happy to just walk out to a hot car." With that, she grabs her purse and heads out of the office.

Erik is coming down the hall and sees her run-walking towards the front door.

"Have fun! Make sure to tell the love of your life I say hello!" She gives him a dismissive wave and pushes through the glass doors.

The cool air is shocking as it hits her face. It has probably dropped twenty degrees since she got to work. She crosses her arms and hurriedly walks to her car. When she's a few feet away, she fishes the keys out of her purse and manually unlocks the door. She swings it open and jumps into the driver seat. She jams the key into the ignition and turns it while buckling her seatbelt with the other hand.

She does pause for a second, just a second, to feel her heart race as the engine fires up.

Every. Single. Time.

She glances at the dashboard clock.

9:25. She gets back on Central Ave but this time heads west on the main road. This will take her right to the highway that leads to Rick's. As soon as she makes her way through town and gets on the open road, she begins her wardrobe change. She unbuckles her seatbelt, slips off her blouse, and pulls on her T-shirt then the hoodie. Next, she steadies the wheel with her thighs as she shimmies off her dress pants and exchanges them for jeans. Not just any jeans, these are her favorite jeans. The only pair of jeans she owns that didn't come from a thrift store.

These are Buckle jeans and they cost $65 of Gabby's hard-earned money. She figured that with making minimum wage, after taxes were taken out, after the 10% tithe to the church and her mandatory 50% from every check going to savings, these jeans totaled about thirty hours of work. They cost more than the rest of her wardrobe combined.

And they were worth it.

They fit PERFECTLY. Not too tight, but not too loose.

They have the perfect wash. Not too light, but not too dark.

And they have just the right amount of destruction. Cute but not ratty.

She loves these jeans.

Finally, she swaps out her black high heels for socks and tennis shoes. She turns off the highway and begins navigating the gravel roads leading to Rick's. There are steep shoulders on each side of the already-narrow roads and the rolling hills add an extra element of difficulty, the benefit to driving them in the dark is that she can cruise right up the middle, knowing that oncoming headlights will warn her of any approaching cars. She's more than halfway there now and she glances again at the clock. She should have about an hour and a half at his house before she'll need to leave to make it home in time for curfew. That's not long, but it should still be enough time... Enough time for what exactly?

She spent so much time trying to finagle a later curfew to make the date last longer, she let herself get excited about it, but she hadn't actually thought about what it would entail. Talking? They'd known each other for year; they didn't have just a whole lot in common.

But that's what first dates are for, right? To talk, to get to know each other. Surely he doesn't expect anything physical to happen... right? It is their first real date... but what if he does?

He is older. He is good-looking. He has those piercing blue eyes. From all she knows about him, and the girls he's dated in the past, he's not a... rookie. She is. She's never... played ball before.

There are many reasons she's never ventured into this particular sporting arena. Obviously, Don's rules hinder extracurricular activities. Throw in Jude's over-protectiveness and that's probably enough to account for her lack of involvement. But those reasons are secondary.

There was the night with Ken, that feeling of helplessness that she actively avoided ever feeling again. But the main deterrent, she knows, is the same thing that dominates most of her life choices. Heck, it's the same thing that shaped her whole personality. *The incident.*

The incident, as Gabby mentally refers to it, was actually a series of events.

Unfortunately, it's not an uncommon scenario.

It began shortly before Seth was born, the beginning of the summer before Gabby started Kindergarten. New neighbors moved in beside the Marksons and the Smiths seemed to be the picture-perfect family. The husband, Lance, was a construction worker and his wife, Laura, was a nurse who worked the night shift. Laura's schedule wasn't ideal but the pay was great and it eliminated the need for childcare for their daughter Annie, who was a year older than Gabby.

The girls hit it off immediately. The day the Smith's moved in, Annie came over to the Markson's backyard to play dolls with Gabby while Don helped them unload their U-haul trailer and Sara brought lemonade out to everyone. The girls played together almost every day for the rest of the summer. The parents also became fast friends. They met up almost weekly to play cards. The girls would be playing dolls or watching TV and they could hear the bursts of laughter from the adults gathered around the kitchen table. Lance was witty and would have the other three in stitches with a well-timed quip or sometimes a single word.

After Seth was born, the get-togethers became less and less frequent.

He was a fussy baby and kept Sara up most of the night. The girls begged for Annie to sleep over at the Markson's, but with the new baby, Sara had to say no. She was afraid Seth would keep the girls up all night. Laura offered to let Gabby stay at their place, but Sara was hesitant. Gabby had never stayed overnight with anyone except family. Sara thanked Laura but declined the offer. However, after a few weeks of little to no sleep (and Gabby's persistent asking) Sara consulted Don and finally gave in. After all, Gabby would be right next door. If anything happened, they could be there in minutes.

Laura made that first sleep over a big deal. She built the girls a fort in the living room. She served them a picnic dinner on a blanket in the living room consisting of grilled cheese sandwiches and cut up apples. Then they stayed up 'really late' (til almost nine o'clock)!

Gabby had a blast. The next morning, Sara was anxiously waiting in their kitchen when Gabby raced in, talking 100 mph telling Sara step-by-step how wonderful the night had been and ending with the french toast smorgasbord Laura prepared for breakfast.

Gabby couldn't wait to do it again.

That afternoon, Laura came over for coffee and the mom's decided that the girls could have a few more sleepovers before school started.

Over the next two weeks, Gabby stayed over eight times. Each time she came home just as excited as she had been that first 'fort night' even though they quickly shifted from forts in the living room to a makeshift mattress for Gabby beside Annie's bed.

The girls started school and both families agreed to limit the sleepovers to weekends. Since Laura worked overnights, Annie stayed at the Markson's the first couple months.

This was fine, but with the two little boys and all her regular toys, Gabby wasn't as excited as when she got to stay at Annie's house. When it came up in conversation, Laura assured Sara it wasn't an issue if the girls wanted to stay at their place. After all, she didn't have to leave for work until 6:50 and the girls usually went to bed at eight. Surely Lance could handle them for an hour... Gabby was elated when Sara told her to pack her bag for the night.

So began the tradition of alternating weekends.

It didn't start right away ~ but Gabby vividly remembers the first time *it* happened.

The first time Lance laid down beside her.

She had been sleeping and woke up to his breath on her face. He said he had a special snack for her in the kitchen. She groggily crawled off the pallet and stumbled out of the bedroom, down the short hallway, and into the dark kitchen. He handed her an unwrapped candy bar that was sitting on the counter.

"Here ya go." He smiled as she hesitantly took the candy bar from his hand.

"Well? Aren't you going to eat it?" He prompted. Still smiling.

Gabby looked at the treat in her hand. She could smell the chocolate. She took a deep breath through her nose and savored the smell. It was a Milky Way. Her favorite.

"I'm not supposed to have candy before bed. It'll rot my... *yawn* ... teeth." She yawned again and rubbed her eyes with her free hand. She was so sleepy. She felt like this was a dream.

Lance smiled at her knowingly, like he'd been expecting her to say that. "It's just a reward for being such a good girl tonight." He paused, "It'll be our little secret."

Gabby took a deep breath and then a big bite.

Heavenly.

She let the chocolate and caramel swirl around her tongue as she chewed. She had her eyes closed (both because she was tired and also because she was savoring the taste of the delicious treat.) When she opened them, Lance had moved closer to her, and his flannel pajama pants were around his ankles. "Now that you've had your secret treat, I have a game for us to play."

He stretched out his hand and caressed her cheek, then tilted her chin up so she would look him in the eyes. "You wanna play a game, don't you?"

Twenty minutes later, after the game, he tucked Gabby back into her makeshift pallet next to Annie's bed. He bent over her, kissed her forehead, and whispered in her ear, "Remember, this is our secret. If you tell anyone about our game, I'll tell your mom you were eating candy before bed." And he patted her head and walked away.

Gabby didn't sleep that night.

The next morning, she went home before breakfast. She walked into her house and went right to her bed where she stayed all day. But she wasn't able to sleep at all.

Every time she closed her eyes she saw... she saw things no six year old should see. The night played in her mind like a video on repeat. The next time it was Gabby's turn to stay at Annie's she came up with an excuse not to stay over... and the next time and the next time. One week she pretended to be sick. The next week she asked her mom if her new friend

Caroline could stay at their house. Annie's feelings were hurt that Gabby suddenly didn't want to be her friend anymore.

Sara began asking Gabby why she didn't want to stay over. She thought the girls had finally worn out the newness of the friendship or that Gabby's new friend Caroline was replacing Annie, Gabby denied both but was terrified to tell anyone the actual reason.

She wasn't just scared of getting in trouble for the candy bar; she knew their game was wrong. She didn't want Sara to be mad at her. Annie pleaded with Gabby to stay over. Tears filled her eyes as she asked why Gabby didn't want to be her friend anymore.

So, Gabby stayed over again.

And again, Lance came in. This time, Gabby felt more emotions. At first it was shame, now she had guilt too. She felt like, since she had been expecting it, that somehow she was asking for it to happen.

And it did.

Over and over.

Each time Gabby felt more and more guilt, more and more shame. She should know better than to come over. Was there something wrong with her? Was it her fault this kept happening?

Each time, after both girls were asleep, Lance would wake Gabby and take her to a different part of the house. The game changed as she got older. Lance introduced different variations.

Gabby hated them all.

At first, she cried every time. Not sobs, but whimpers. She cried... but he always gave her a Milky Way afterwards. Eventually she learned to turn off her mind. To not think. She learned to detach herself from the scared little girl who was being hurt. Eventually Gabby was able to watch what was happening like a movie and then put it in a box when it was over.

What she couldn't figure out was how to erase it.

The images would run through her mind constantly.

After a few months Gabby felt so guilty it would make her physically sick to her stomach.

As the girls got older their sleepovers became less and less frequent. They made other friends and Annie became involved with sports, but they still slept over on occasion. And every time, Lance would wake Gabby up. Then, when she was ten years old, it just stopped. Gabby laid on the floor of Annie's room, staring at the ceiling, waiting for Lance to beckon her for their game.

But he never came.

When she stayed over a couple weeks later, she was left alone again. It stopped. Just like that. But Gabby still hated going to their house and made excuses not to stay overnight.

She was relieved when Annie told her that they were moving. Gabby would miss her friend but she hoped that now she would be able to forget... everything.

Gabby kept their secret.

She never told a soul.

To this day she can't smell that candy bar without bile rising in her throat.

And that's not the only side effect; all these years later, when Gabby is put in a position that reminds her of 'game night' her body will physically react.

She gets a pit in her stomach, her heart races, and her mind screams for her to run or shut down.

Most of the time she shuts down, then boxes up. This process had protected her as an innocent child from fully experiencing the pain and horror that coincide with abuse, but it hindered the emotional development of the adolescent. Now that Gabby is well into her teen years, there are a lot built up emotions that she has packed away.

CHAPTER 17

Gabby turns onto the long winding driveway that leads to the two-story farmhouse. Her heart begins to beat faster and her breathing becomes shallow. Why is she so anxious... or is this excited? Either way, she needs to calm down. She pulls her car off to the side, not really on a driveway, but just a section of the lawn that has doubled as parking so many times there are two parallel strips of dead grass. Gabby puts the car in park, takes a couple deep breaths through her nose and does a quick once over in the mirror. She tugs at the hair-tie that is holding her mess of brown hair back in a ponytail. Pulling it free, her hair falls over her shoulders and the natural curls frame her face.

She slides her tongue over her teeth checking for lodged popcorn kernels. None, good.

She wishes she had lipstick or mascara or... something. Something to help her not look so... plain.

But she doesn't. Al' natural is gonna have to do. Per usual.

She cups her hand in front of her mouth and blows into it while inhaling through her nose, trying to smell her own breath. Nothing. She's not sure if that's good or bad. Should she have a mint? Gum? 'Cause she doesn't.

Gabby grabs her lipstickless, mascraless, mintless, gumless, pointless purse, and turns the ignition off.

Now that she is sufficiently self-conscience, Gabby pushes the car door open and walks to the front entry. She rings the bell and nervously shifts from one foot to the other.

It's unseasonably chilly out tonight and her sweatshirt isn't warm. She wraps her arms around her body and turns against the cold wind. The door suddenly swings open and she's greeted by Rick's smiling face. She hadn't thought it was possible, but her heart started beating even faster.

"Hey," His smile is revealing that dang dimple, she looks into those twinkling blue eyes and she's no longer cold.

"Hey," She smiles back and steps inside as he opens the door wider. He looks fantastic. She has known him for years; has he always looked this good? Or is it her imagination? He's wearing a loose-fitting T-shirt and faded jeans with holes up and down both legs. But the thing that's making her knees actually shake is that he smells amazing. It's a mixture of soap, Aqua de Gio, and... something she couldn't quite decipher. Raw manliness? Whatever it is, Gabby's a fan.

She steps further into the familiar farmhouse and takes a deep breath. His cologne mixes with the usual aromas of their home. Lemon pine-sol, fresh laundry, and lavender.

Gabby has been in this house a number of times. Her parents are good friends of Ricks' parents and they love playing cards during the winter and having bonfires in the summer. She's been here with her family often, but this time is different.

Rick puts his hand on the small of her back and guides her into the living room. The heat of his hand radiates through her sweatshirt and she imagines it branding her back. She is aware of her steps, her breathing, her nerves, everything. She is hyper aware of everything.

The television is turned on to MTV. "Did you wanna watch a movie or ....?" He lets the sentence trail off.

"Uh, actually, this is fine." She shrugs towards the TV where the group of party people are at a bar, making terrible choices. "But..ummm... I, uh, can't stay too long." She stammers.

She hates that she's so nervous. It's Rick.

"Cool. You want somethin' to drink?" He motions for her to sit.

"Yeah, um, water would be awesome."

"You got it." He disappears around the corner to the kitchen. She drops her purse on the end table, pulls her hoodie over her head, and tosses it on top of her purse before settling down at the end of the couch.

For the love of all things holy, Gabrielle, get a hold of yourself. For crying out loud, what is your problem?

It's Rick. Yes, he is a boy. Yes, he is attractive. But you're acting like you've never held a conversation before. Quit being an idiot.

She closes her eyes, empties her chest of all the air, trying to cleanse her nervousness.

She's positive Rick can hear her heart beating. Why is she so nervous? She crosses and recrosses her legs, fidgeting.

Rick reappears carrying two glasses of ice water. He sets them on the table in front or her, grabs the remote that had been tossed on a recliner in the corner (probably where he was sitting before she got here) and walks back over to the couch.

He sits down next to her, so close that the outside of their thighs are touching and Gabby is surrounded by an invisible cloud of his musk. That knee-knocking aroma.

If she thought her heart was beating fast before, well now, it found a mallet and was hammering it into her chest.
Her palms are sweating and, all of a sudden, she is very worried about how she smells. Her popcorn and theater grime probably mix nicely with her un-minty breath.

Meanwhile, he smells like Abercrombie and Fitch with a stick of Spearmint.

She glances at him and he is looking at her expectantly. Had he asked her a question?

"Uh.. Um.. What?"

He smiles, amused by how nervous she is, "I just asked how your folks were doin'."

"Oh. They're fine."

Well, this first date where they learn all about each other is going swell.

Gabby is so frustrated with herself. Why can't she chill?

Then Caroline's voice echoes in her head, "You have got to be kidding me. Get. A. Grip. You're embarrassing yourself. You are better than this." And with that, a smile plays across Gabby's lips and she actually settles into the couch for the first time.

This is Rick. Yes, he is gorgeous. Yes, he smells amazing. It is still Rick.

"So, my brother's hamster finally died. But it's ok. He was way past his prime. He actually left a pretty impressive lineage..." and she went into the story about how he had fathered the entire northern Iowa hamster population in 2000. She quickly tells about how they initially got Wafer, and his 'brother' Vanilla... but it turned out Vanilla was a female. They discovered this after she had her first litter.

They tried to sell the hamster babies but they grew quickly and before they knew it, the Marksons were operating an unsanctioned hamster farm against their will. When they finally were able to give away all the generations, Sara demanded Vanilla go too. Only Wafer would remain.

They both laughed and Rick slid his arm behind her back. Her heart raced, but this time she embraces it, and leans her head back into his shoulder.

They watch the bar scene on the TV and it reminds her of something funny Randy said about one of her customers. When Gabby turns her head to tell Rick, he meets her halfway and softly kisses her lips.

Her mind races. Then he moves his hand to her cheek and gently places her face in his palm, and her mind finally goes blank.

She lets herself feel the goosebumps rising on her arms.

She lets the butterflies flit around in her stomach.

She lets herself feel her heart soar.

She lets herself enjoy this magical moment.

Their first kiss.

Then he puts his other hand on her thigh.

That's when the butterflies in her stomach are replaced with the black pit.

Lance's face flashes in her mind. The joy and expectancy of another kiss is replaced by bile rising in her throat. She squeezes her eyes tightly shut, trying to erase the images that are flooding her thoughts.

She opens them to see Rick looking at her, concern creasing his face. Her cheeks flush. She fidgets with her phone, nervously spinning it in her hands.

"I'm sorry, it's just..."

That's when she notices the time.

"Shoot!!! I gotta go!" And with that, she grabs her purse and heads for the door.

A very confused Rick grabs her sweatshirt from the couch and follows her outside. Gabby is already in the car so he leans in the driver's side window.

Gabby can't bring herself to look at him so she stares at the steering wheel, "I'm sorry, I really can't be late."

He hands her the sweatshirt through the window and says, "It's ok."

She tosses the hoodie in the passenger seat as she turns on the ignition.

She revs the engine and does a quick three-point turn in the driveway and guns it back onto the gravel road.

Glancing in the rear-view mirror, she sees Rick standing on the corner of the lawn, under their yard light, one hand in his pocket, the other gives her a quick wave.

Dang it. That's not how she wanted the night to end.

Dang it, dang it, dang it.

She looks at the clock again as she tops the first hill.

She's a few minutes behind schedule but she can still make it home on time.

If she hurries.

CHAPTER 18

Nick stares at his phone.

12:05... He knows Gabby has a midnight curfew.
He should call her. Just to see how she's doing.
He has been playing the conversation possibilities over and over in his mind.

"Hey Gabby.... I'm madly in love with you."

Or "Yo... Gabbs, listen up..."

Or "Hey gurrllll. What's up."

Or true Joey Tribioni style, "How you doin?"

This is ridiculous, it's Gabby. He'll figure it out.
He highlights her number and quickly presses send before he loses his nerve.

He hears the first ring...

CHAPTER 19

Blackness.
Cold.
Dark.
A ringing that sounds far away.
My mind recognizes the noise, but I can't place it.
Blackness.
Cold.
Dark.
The ringing again... this time it's closer.
The ringing stirs in the back of my conscious.
I open my eyes against the darkness.
I'm freezing.
I force my eyes open as the ringing starts again.
My phone. It's my cell phone.
I can feel everything, it's like my nerves are raw, exposed.
Where am I? Think Gabrielle.
I can feel hard earth underneath me.
I can feel the wind whipping through my bones.
I can feel the hair on my head, weighing down my skull.
I can feel a knife-like pain ripping through my head.

I can feel every goose-bump on my body like each one is an individual sensor.

My body feels like it's covered in a sheet of frost.

I'm freezing, shivering from head to toe.

Again, I hear my phone ringing, but I can't see anything.

I stare straight up into the night sky, willing my eyes to focus.

I turn my head toward the sound and my body erupts with bursts of pain.

My brain is only registering one thought at a time.

Right now, PAIN is dominating.

I need to block it out so I can figure out what's going on.

It's dark, it's cold, and my face hurts.

It feels like I'm laying on rocks.

Oh, I am actually laying on rocks.

WHY am I laying on rocks?

My eyes finally begin to adjust.

I try to sit up and look for my phone.

The waves of pain knock me back over.

Every muscle, every bone, every inch of my skin hurts.

Everything. Everything hurts.

What. In. The. Heck. is going on?!?!?

My phone rings again, it's gotta be almost the last one before whoever is calling gets sent to voice-mail or hangs up.

I take a deep breath, hoist myself up to my elbows and, as quickly as I can, I roll over onto my knees.

My eyes are watering and they sting.

I still can't see clearly.

I lean back on my haunches and openly sob from the pain.

I try to wipe away the tears that are cascading down my face, but my hand brushes against, what feels like scales, instead of my smooth cheeks. Very painful scales.

What happened?!?!

Where am I?!?!

The fog in my mind is beginning to clear and I am now sufficiently freaking out.

I know I'm outside, obviously.

I still can't completely see, and it's not just the darkness. My eyes sting but they're starting to adjust.

Where is my phone???

I'm sitting in the middle of a gravel road.

I know I'm in the country. I think there's a house in the distance, but I can't really make it out.

I see what looks appears to be a porch light. I finally spot my phone as it begins the shrill ring again.

It's upside down on the side of the road, maybe 20 feet away.

Again, I try to stand up but immediately fall back down.

I'm beginning to see a pattern here.

Now, thanks to a combination of pain and fear, I start sobbing again.

WHAT HAPPENED?!!?

UGH! I hate crying. Get it together Gabby.

Go Gabby. Go. Get the phone.

I stop the tears, brace myself against the excruciating pain that I know is coming, and start to crawl toward the familiar ringtone.

With every inch if feels like thousands of tiny needles are pricking me from my thighs to my toes. My hands are raw and it hurts so badly to put weight on them. I try to alternate the pressure between the pinpricking in my legs and the blinding pain in my hands as I lock my eyes straight ahead on the phone. Just get there. Go. It feels like I crossed the length of a football field, but in reality, it was only a few yards. I collapse next to the phone, grab it, and turn it over.

The cover is gone.

My phone is a basic 2002 Nokia, the back is a battery, then there's a separate keypad, and finally a cover. Normally, my phone sports a bright yellow faceplate riddled with palm trees and parrots, but now the cover and keypad are nowhere in sight.

Luckily, the battery is still intact, so I start furiously pushing down on the spot where the answering button is supposed to be.

"Hello?!? Hello?!?!?" What is the matter with my voice? It's high, squeaky, and frantic.

"Gabby? Gabby are you ok?" It's Nick.

"NICK! I don't know what I happened. I don't know where I am. I am so scared!" The words are pouring out of my mouth.

"Ok. It's ok. Gabby, where are you?" I hear the concern in his voice as he tries to calm me down.

"I DON'T KNOW! I can't remember anything. I don't know where I am, I don't know where I was..." I can't breathe. I sit up to get air in my lungs, I try to cross my legs, but either they are in shock or my brain isn't relaying the message. Whichever it is, I have to use my free hand to move both legs in, crossing them in front of me so I can lean forward, expanding my belly and lungs.

"Gabby! Gabby, calm down. I'm going to hang up. You need to call your parents."

"NO! WAIT! I can't! My phone is busted!" Hysterical. I've always wondered what it would feel like to be hysterical. Now I know.

Oh. My. Word. Gabrielle Faith Markson, pull yourself together.

Deep Breath

Calm down.

Deep Breath

Calm down.

...Nope, can't do it. I guess I'll play this hysteria thing out.

I try to at least talk slowly, but the words tumble out of my mouth at rapid speed and I can't stop them.

"Nick, I think I was in a car accident. I'm not sure what happened but my phone is busted." The more I talk, the more worked up I get. "It's dark. I'm freezing. I'm hurt. Nick, I'm scared."

"It's ok. You're gonna be ok. Do you know where you are?"

"NO! I told you, I don't rememb-"

"Ok, I'm gonna call your dad." Click.

He hung up. I stare at the bloody remnant of my phone. Blood has seeped into the openings where the keys are supposed to be.

I'm all alone.

Again.

It'll be fine.

Nick will call my dad and my dad will come find me.

It'll be fine.

I can't breathe. It's so cold.

I cross my arms to try to keep warm but it feels like needles scraping across my bare skin. I look down to see my arms are both caked in blood.

What. The. Heck.

I touch my face, and it's hard.

My face feels hard.

Why, why does my face feel hard?!?!

Panic is rising in my chest. For the first time, the pieces are clicking.

I was scared before but the realization that something terrible actually happened hits me like a lead weight.

Anxiety washes over me.

Ok, I need to clear my thoughts.

Another deep breath and I shake my head, like I'm physically shaking the thoughts out... but as I turn my head to the side, I feel my scalp move.

MY SCALP JUST MOVED.

Slowly, I bring my shaking hand up to my head.

I gingerly feel around the area that is aching and my fingers slide under my hair, into my head.

MY FINGERS ARE INSIDE MY HEAD.

The warmth of blood engulfs three of my fingers up to the knuckle and begins running down my arm, I yank my hand back and a suction sound rings in my ears as my scalp slaps back down.

I think I'm going to throw up.

My head starts spinning and I'm dizzy.

A black fog starts to creep in and all I want to do it close my eyes...

No! No. I need to stay awake.

I need to figure out what's going on.

CHAPTER 20

Don wakes from a dead sleep and grabs at the phone ringing by his head. The cord twists as he fumbles with it, finally getting it to his ear he says, "Yeah... Hello?"

His voice is gruff, still heavy with sleep. He looks at the clock on his nightstand. 12:23 a.m.

"Hello Mr. Markson, my name is Nick Tanner. I'm sorry to wake you. I'm a friend of Gabby's. She wanted me to call to tell you she was in a car accident."

Now Don is wide awake. His heart beats out of his chest. He sits up, swinging his legs over the side of the bed, and jostles Sara awake with his arm.

"Gabby? Where is she? Is she ok?"

"Yeah, yeah, I think she's ok... Umm. I'm not sure where she is, she just said somewhere on the side of the road, I think. But she wasn't sure where but she needs you to come get her."

"Ok, we're leaving now. Thank you." Don hangs up the phone and grabs a pair of jeans and a jacket as his panic from before is slowly being replaced with anger.

Leave it to Gabby to concoct such a scheme.

"What's going on?" Sara is out of bed, but she's waiting on her husband to fill her in as to why.

"Gabby's late. She had a friend call to say she is on the side of the road."

Sara's face goes pale.

"Calm down," Don reassures her. "If it were bad the police would have called. Gabby probably knew she was going to miss curfew and didn't want to get grounded again so she called a friend and had him call me. I'll go find her, drive her out of whatever ditch she has parked in, and be home in an hour."

"I'm going with you, just in case." Sara had already gotten dressed and was grabbing a blanket out of their closet. Don shrugs, grabs his cellphone and his wallet, and they head out the door. They hop in the minivan and he dials Gabby's cell phone from his own as they back out of the driveway.

This girl will be the death of him. She never ceases to amaze him, just when he thinks he's onto whatever tricks she may have, she pulls something like this.

They head toward Ellesburg.

She better have been at Rick's.

CHAPTER 21

After having my hand inside my head, and my scalp making noises, I decide I need to lie back down.

I need to calm myself. I gingerly uncross my legs and lean back slowly.

On the rocks.

In the dark.

All alone.

I feel emotions swirling around inside me like never before.

Fear is the main one. It's bursting through my seams.

Anxiety is close behind.

There's also loneliness.

But mostly fear. I'm so scared I can't think straight. I can actually see red flashing lights in my head. My brain needs to shut down the fear. I need to shut down. Turn off.

Lying on the road, surrounded by darkness, shivering, I close my eyes and my mind goes into autopilot.

I start to build a box. My breathing slows down as I imagine a dark blue base, I can see 360 degrees around it, and I begin to add the sides, all the same color as the base, one at a time. Once I have the four walls solidly built on the base, I rotate it in my mind. Seeing it empty. Seeing it secure. Then I imagine scooping up all the fear swirling around in my head, packing it down and placing it in the box. Then taking a lid and covering the box. A padlock appears on the front and I spin the dial.

My lungs empty into the cold air and I feel lighter.

Next, the anxiety. My mind produces another base, this one is forest green.

I begin to build the walls...

My phone rings. Snapping me from my meditation.

I roll onto my side, grimacing in pain, and hit the blood-soaked spot where the answer key should be as I push myself back up into a sitting position.

"Hello?!?!?!"

"Gabrielle Faith Markson, where are you?" Dad's voice crackles through the phone.

He is not happy.

"I don't know." I'm much calmer now than I was when Nick called. My body still screams with pain, but my mind is quieter.

I can think.

"What do you mean you don't know? Were you at Ricks?"

"I don't remember."

"What do you mean you don't remember?"

"I don't know. I don't know where I am. I don't know where I was. I don't know what I was doing." Now that I am starting to think straight, I look around to try to get my bearings. If I'm going to have a confrontation with my dad, I'm going to be armed with some info.

First things first; Where am I?

I turn around to get a full picture of my surroundings, and for the first time, I see my car.

My precious Berretta.

Upside down.

Well, now I know what happened.

The sight of my pride and joy crumpled into a heap takes my breath away.

I just stare at it.

My car is upside down. I am covered in blood. My whole body is shaking uncontrollably and I'm freezing.

Am I dying?

I think this is what happens when you die. I'm pretty sure you get cold and jittery, then die.

Dad's voice snaps my mind away from these thoughts, back to the task at hand: figuring out where I am.

"Gabrielle Faith!!! I said, are you in Ruthshire?"

The use of my full name is getting old.

"I. Don't. Know."

"What do you see?" Even on the phone his voice is confrontational.

"I see a light." My tone matches his in sharpness. "I think it's a farmhouse. Do you want me to go there?" My words come out more defiant than I intended, but at least the hysteria is gone.

"No. Stay where you are."

Fine. I will. That's what I wanted to do anyway.

My head is killing me.

"Are you in your car?" If he has even a smidgen of concern, he is hiding it well.

"No, I'm on the road. My car is in the ditch." At the mention of my car, I turn towards it.

My mind starts to race again as I feel my heart actually breaking in my chest. I grit my teeth and hoist myself up to a standing position. My legs feel like jello. I don't know if it's the cold wind or the multiple cuts covering my body, but I feel like I have frost bite head to toe.

I feel like a newborn baby giraffe making my way to the car. Wobbling slowly, my dad's voice is a low lull in my ear.

My sweet, sweet, car. I do a mental evaluation of the damage. The windshield is completely crashed in. My driver side window is gone. The front bumper is gone. The whole right side is crumpled. I feel tears fill my eyes again. This time I don't know if it's from the pain or the heartbreak.

"Are your lights on?" Dad's tone commands my attention.

"No." My voice is quieter now, no longer combative.

"Turn your lights on." His still is.

"Ok." I don't even have the energy to fight.

Hmmm... now to figure out how to turn the lights on.

While my dad continues talking about responsibility and punishment, I shift my focus again; I need to turn the lights on... lights on... lights on... well, first I'll need to get the car right side up.

If dad's this upset about me being out here, then he'll be livid if he sees my car like this.

I think one good heave should probably flip this puppy right over.

With dad still yammering in my ear, I prop the phone between my shoulder and my cheek (ouch, ouch, that hurts) but now at least I have both hands to work with.

One, two, three and... fail.

My genius plan to hulk the car over didn't work and now I've actually slid underneath it.

Smart move, Gabby.

141

Come to think of it, I might not be thinking clearly.

Actually, I am pretty dizzy and it feels like my head is in a vise.

I lay my head back with my body still resting underneath my car.

I feel heavy, like I'm sinking into the earth.

"GABBY! Can you see a street sign or anything so I know where you are?" Oh good. We've circled back to the topic of my location. I thought we covered this already.

"No dad. All I see is that light, the road, and dark."

"Did you go to work tonight?... Gabby?... Gabrielle? Did you go to work tonight?" The connection is choppy. I try to reply to him, but my phone is shorting out.

Perfect. The blood must have finally seeped all the way through. Frustration mounts and I move the phone directly in front of my mouth.

"I. DO. NOT. KNOW!"

He matches my frustration with, "Then turn your lights on so we can see you!"

Next, I hear muffled noises and my mom's voice comes on the line.

"Gabby?"

Maybe it is relief from a break of the overwhelming frustration with my dad, maybe it's hearing the concern in her tone, whatever it is, her voice triggers my inner child. I start crying and my voice shifts from defiant and angry to soft and whiny.

"Mama, I'm cold. My head hurts."

"I know Baby Girl; will you please turn your lights on so we can see you?"

"Mom, I can't get to the switch, I tried, but my car's upside down."

Silence.

"Gabby, did you say your car is upside down?"

Had I not mentioned that before?

Ooooohhhhhhhhhhhh...

That little tidbit may have softened dad's tone.

Ah-ha. He probably thinks I drove into the ditch and asked Nick to call him so I wouldn't get it trouble.

That is genius, I wish I woulda thought of that over my birthday weekend...

"Gabby?"

"Yeah mom, I'm here."

"There's a lot of static. Your phone keeps cutting out."

"Mama, I'm scared."

"I know Baby, we're on our -"

"Mom? Mama? Mom?!?!" I yell into the phone but there's nothing. No sound at all.

The phone is completely dead.

Awesome. Ok Gabby. Don't freak out. Keep calm. Stay in control.

Let's take a quick inventory of our surroundings, shall we?

I'm still lodged under the car from my failed attempt to 'flip this puppy over'. Luckily, I slid in pretty seamlessly so I'm not so much stuck as I am just lying underneath it.

I could wait here... but as I lay my head back down, I see something out of the corner of my eye.

Is that...?

It is.

Bessie. The stuffed cow Jude gave me for my birthday a couple months ago.

I love that cow, I keep her in my car because she makes me smile.

Now she's a few yards away in the ditch.

143

Stacey Spangler

Is it worth the effort to go all the way over there?

Yes. Yes it is.

I manage to wiggle my butt back and use the car as leverage to hoist myself up. I use my beloved Beretta as a handrail to slowly make my way towards Bessie. I barely wobble over to her, on legs that feel like blobs of goo being supported by fickle fish bones, but when I bend down to pick her up, I lose my balance and fall forward doing a clumsy (and very painful) somersault. I land on my back and now I'm on the side of the ditch facing the road.

You know what? This is good. I'll wait here.

I curl my knees up to my chest, wrap my arms around my legs, lay my head on Bessie and focus on staying warm.

My mind is surprisingly clear.

I'm covered in blood, my entire body is shaking so violently I feel like I'll bounce across the road, but I can think, so I pray, "Dear God, please let me live."

And as soon as I utter the words, everything is crystal clear.

All the months of inner dialog, explained.

All the self-doubt, vanished.

The struggle of the two Gabby's, resolved. Now they are aligned perfectly.

I smile, my heart feeling lighter than I ever remember, and   I   close   my   eyes.

CHAPTER 22

The line goes dead.

"Gabby!!!" Sara screams into the Don's phone, clutching it in her hands, but the only reply is a dial tone. She hangs up and quickly calls Gabby's phone again, but it goes straight to voice-mail; "Hey it's Gabby. I'm either at school, working, or grounded from my phone. Leave me a message, or better yet, just text me."

Sara looks over at her husband. All the color has drained from his face and his eyes are wide, focused on the road.

"Her car's upside down?" He asks the question as a statement.

Upside down.

Sara nods, staring blankly ahead.

Don's entire body feels like someone just tightened it with a vice. Every muscle, every nerve is completely taught.

How had this happened? How had their relationship become so tense, so distant, so strained that his first reaction was one of distrust and anger?

Gabby has been pushing him away for months and he's been scrapping and pushing to get back in, now when she needed him, he lectured instead of listened.

That is changing right now.

He'll apologize to Gabby.

He'll make it right.

All he's ever wanted was to protect her. This parenting thing is harder than he ever imagined.

"Don?" Sara's voice is quivering but even.

"She'll be fine. She'll be fine," he reassures her but even as he does, he accelerates even more. They are flying down the highway well over 80 mph but Sara isn't complaining. They can't get there fast enough.

Don's mind races: Gabby. Why does he assume the worst in her? Why is his first reaction always so harsh? He had been certain this was one of her stunts. Mainly because he can't even begin to imagine something bad actually happening to her.

His hands are shaking but he does his best to not show his wife how terrified he is.

His beautiful bride is staring straight ahead, scanning for signs of their daughter.

She is composed, not hysterical. Calm in the face of calamity. One of the many fantastic qualities he loves about her. One of the many she passed onto their daughter.
Their Gabby. He barely slows down as he makes the turn off the blacktop, then he presses the gas pedal to the floor and the minivan jolts as it kicks up gravel.

He prays Gabby is here, that she is where she was supposed to be.

CHAPTER 23

Headlights! I see headlights! And they're headed this way.

It's gotta be my parents.

With Bessie firmly in hand I start crawling down the ditch towards the road just as our minivan comes to a stop.

Dad jumps out the driver door, talking on his cell phone, and runs back the way they just came.

Mom runs to me. She's carrying a blanket and she wraps it around me as crouches next to me.

I feel myself melt into her and start sobbing and shaking uncontrollably. I have zero strength left.

I can feel mom holding me but I'm not sure of much else.

Dad is back, he's kneeling in front of me. He's crying. And he's praying.

My body feels heavy, but also light.

I feel like I'm drifting in and out of sleep.

Maybe I'm losing consciousness, but would I know? Do you know when you're unconscious?

I wonder what time it is?

Even with the blanket around me and mom holding me, I'm freezing.

The energy I had when I was on the phone with dad is completely gone. I can't move at all, my brain is telling my arm to hug my mom but every appendage feels like it weighs roughly a million pounds.

All I can do is lean into her.

Maybe I'll just close my eyes for a second...

I must have dozed off because the next thing I know, I'm abruptly woken by a flashlight shining in my eyes.

"Have you been drinking?"

I don't recognize the voice and I can't see a face because of the laser light in my eyes, but I see the flashing lights of a police car pulled in behind the van so I'm assuming this is a police officer.

"Have you been drinking?" He repeats the question.

I try to shake my head but it hurts too much so I muster up, "No."

I do a lot of stupid things but drinking and driving is not one of them.

It doesn't matter that I can't remember where I was or what I was actually doing, I know I wasn't drinking if I had to drive home.

"Were you driving?" There is not a trace of sympathy in his voice. I can't see what I look like, but judging by the way I feel, I'd guess I look like I was just in a car accident.

That doesn't faze this guy. Again he asks, "Were you the driver?"

Again, I try to answer by nodding my head, again it hurts too much so I say, "Yeah." But it even feels weird to talk.

Every time I open my mouth, my face moves.

It feels like I'm wearing an ill-fitting (and extremely painful) Halloween mask.

"Was there anyone else in the car?" This guy. He doesn't let up, does he?

"I don't think so."

The police officer turns on a dime and starts walking up and down the ditch, sweeping his flashlight to scan the area. I want to give him the benefit of the doubt that he's looking for other passengers, but I'm assuming he's looking for the beer cans I know he won't find.

I see more lights and hear a siren. I'm hoping this is an ambulance and not another police officer. I need a couple band-aids, not more questions.

Thank God. Literally, Thank You Jesus, it's an ambulance.

It screeches to a stop almost right in front of us.

Two people jump out of the back doors before it even comes to a complete stop, and then they're joined by a third. I'm guessing he's the driver.

"Hi honey, what's your name?" It's a female EMT. She crouches down beside me and takes my hand.

"Gabby."

"Ok, good, good. Do you know what happened?" A male EMT kneels in front of me. Hey, I know him. It's Jason (the older brother of a friend of mine) asking the million-dollar question.

"I'm not sure." Everything is spinning. I feel like I'm going to puke.

I take a deep breath and try to push away the vomiting sensation. I close my eyes to concentrate on not throwing up on everyone but then I can't open them again.

I don't think I can talk anymore. Thankfully, mom takes over so I don't have to.

"We got a call from one of her friends who told us she was in an accident. We found her about 10 minutes ago and my husband called 911. She can't remember anything. We don't know what happened."

With my eyes still closed I hear Jason say, "Okay kiddo, we're gonna take you to the hospital to get you fixed up."

Suddenly I feel two sets of hands on me, then I hear counting, then they hoist me onto a stretcher.

One, two, and three.

Ouch, ouch, and ouch.

The pain is reaching every inch of my body. The warm, brightly lit inside of the ambulance is a stark contrast to the cold darkness outside. I hear the doors shut and we start to move. It takes all my strength to open my eyes for a few seconds.

"Where's my mom?" I ask aloud but to no one in particular.

Jason answers, "She'll meet us at the hospital. Gabby, I'm going to ask you some questions. I need you to stay awake, ok?"

No deal. Sleep is literally the only thing I want to do.

It hurts to breathe.

It hurts even more to talk.

I'll answer your questions but I'm not opening my eyes. Non-negotiable.

I nod, agreeing to the questions, not the awake part.

"Gabby, how old are you?"

Oh, we're diving right into the questions.

Good.

"Seventeen." I manage in a voice that's no more than a whisper, trying to move my lips as little as possible.

"Awesome, awesome." He mumbles but gaging by the quiver in his voice, I don't think he means it.

The female EMT chimes in, "Gabby, we to need to get a better look at you. I'm going to start cutting your clothes off."

My jeans. My favorite 'make my butt look perfect' jeans. My mourning is cut short because Jason resumes his little interrogation.

"Hey Gabby, where do you go to school?"

I've watched enough TV to know that he's asking me questions to keep me conscious. If you have to ask me questions, at least make them good ones, at least ask me something you might not know the answer to.

"Ruthshire."

"Oh yeah? My little sister goes to Ruthshire. What year are you?"

"Junior." I feel my breaths getting shallower, it's like there is a cinder block on my chest.

"So is she," Jason answers and follows with, "Gabby, Gabby I need you to open your eyes for me."

You know what? He really doesn't seem to know it's me. I force myself to open my eyes one more time and look at him.

"Jason..." the mention of his name startles him, "It's me. Gabby Markson."

I've never seen a person turn this particular shade of white. I've heard the saying about all the color draining from someone's face, but I've never actually seen it. Until now. And let me tell you, it's comforting.

Just kidding. It's not comforting. Not at all.

"Gabby, how do you know Jason?" The female EMT jumps in to cover for the visibly shaken Jason.

"Hissister." The words blend together and I feel my eyes roll back. I hear them talking. I know they're talking about me. Something about blood pressure. I try to stay awake but I can't.

The next thing I know, they're unloading me from the ambulance and it's just like in the movies.

They're yelling out vitals as they push me through the emergency doors and down the hall.

The lady EMT is running next to the stretcher "Seventeen-year-old female, car accident, severe head trauma..."

I don't hear Jason, I hope he's ok.

CHAPTER 24

They held it together until the back doors of the ambulance slammed shut and their daughter was whisked away. Then Sara fell to her knees, her whole body quaking as she cried. Don fought through his own tears to help his wife into the van so they could follow their daughter.

Now Don is laser-focused on maneuvering their minivan as they race around corners, trying to catch up to the swirling blue lights of the ambulance. Sara is in the passenger seat, sobbing into her hands, repeating the same phrase over and over: "My baby girl. My baby girl."

Her mind is racing between images of Gabby as a toddler waddling around with her dogs then flashing to her beautiful face, caked with blood, her scalp flapping open, and her body a heap on the side of the road. Sara, holding her daughter's broken body, trying to stop the bleeding but not even knowing where to begin.

They speed down Central Ave, flying through the flashing stoplights.

By now, it's almost one a.m. and everything is quiet, Don doesn't even bother finding a parking spot as he squeals to a stop in front of the emergency room doors and they run inside.

"My daughter, she's seventeen, she was just brought in." He yells towards the reception counter as the automatic doors are opening.

The receptionist is calm; she looks up at him and simply asks, "Her name?"

"Gabby. Gabrielle Markson."

The receptionist clicks a few keys, looks intently at the screen, and then back to them.

"She's in the emergency room. The doctors are tending to her now."

"Can we see her?" Sara asks, louder than she intended.

The receptionist sighs and says, "I'll see what I can do." This time without looking up from her screen.

Don and Sara hold each other and look around the empty lobby, at a loss of what to do, both let their gaze settle on the red 'Emergency Room' sign.

A nurse heading that direction overheard the exchange and beckons them to follow her. She leads them down a bright hallway and whispers, "You can't stay long, just a moment."

They walk briskly back to the emergency room, they turn the corner and Sara feels all the air leave her lungs.

She sees Gabby.

Her daughter is lying on an operating table, wearing only a bra and panties.

There are nurses and doctors filling the room. There is so much blood surrounding her.

Blood everywhere.

A doctor appears in front of them. With a curt nod in lieu of a greeting, he goes directly into relaying the information with the same sincerity as if he were a fast-food worker reading back a drive through order. Sara hears the words, but her brain refuses to process them.

"She's lost a lot of blood. A lot. Her body is covered with multiple abrasions, obviously the most concerning is the head wound. Next is the gash on her right leg. It's extremely deep, all the way to the bone and dangerously close to an artery. We can't tell yet if there's muscle damage. She's going to need an MRI and cat scan to see if there's internal bleeding or swelling. We think we have the bleeding from her head under control, for now. The most immediate concern is swelling around the brain."

Then he says the sentence that will play over and over in her mind. "The next couple hours are critical. If she survives, we will know more in the morning." Then he turns and walks away.

If? IF??? IF she survives?!?!!?

The nurse reappears from behind the doctor and offers to show them to the waiting room. She has large brown eyes, shoulder-length blond hair, and a kind face. She takes Sara's arm and speaks in a low tone, trying to offer words of comfort, "Be thankful it was so cold, that slowed down the bleeding. Be thankful for the call, another hour she would've been gone."

They walked the short distance down the hall before coming to the waiting room. It's a small, bare room with only four chairs lined up against each of the four walls.

"I'll come get you when she's out of surgery." The nice nurse turns to leave but quickly adds, "We're short-staffed tonight. I'll do my best to keep you updated but I can't make any promises." Then she too turns, and rushes back down the empty hallway.

The couple is alone in the quiet waiting room. There is a TV in the corner but it is turned off. The florescent lighting flickers and one is already burned out in the corner. Sara turns into Don and he holds his wife as she cries.

What now? What are they supposed to do while a team of medical professionals work to save their daughter? Don leads Sara over to two chairs in the darker corner under the burned-out light. They sit together, elbows on their knees, heads in the hands, both praying.

Sara pleads with God to spare her child; Don bargains with God, offering anything and everything in exchange for Gabby's life.

Half an hour later, with puffy eyes and heavy hearts, they start making calls.

Sara's voice is monotone as she calls her mom and a couple ladies from church. Her speech is the same as she paces around the small waiting room.

"Sorry to wake you, we need your prayers. Gabby was in a car accident. We're at the hospital now. I'll call you when we know more."

Don also makes his calls, circling counterclockwise to Sara. His parents, his brother, and a few close friends. His spiel is the same as his wife's. Almost word for word. After they both hang up the last of the calls, they embrace again.

There are no more tears. Sara is anxious, Don holds her. Both their minds swirling. They have a longer list of calls to make in a few hours, when it's not in the middle of the night.

Caroline and Jude will want to know. Sara makes a mental note to figure out a way to call to thank Nick. The name sounds familiar, but she cannot picture his face. Her mind was mush.

"What should we do about the boys?" Don whispers in her ear. Her sons haven't been far from her mind all night.

"I think you should go get them and tell them what happened. They will want to be here."

Don knows she's right but hates the thought of leaving her alone, but he expects other members of their family to arrive shortly.

"Okay, I'll go get them, text me as soon as you know anything." He gives his wife one more squeeze and a kiss on the forehead.

"She's going to be okay." He gives her what he hopes is a confident look and repeats again, as much for himself as for his wife, "She's going to be okay." Then he rushes out the door.

CHAPTER 25

Randy is being heckled by a table of drunk outta-towners when she sees an ambulance fly past the front window of Frank's, speeding down Central.

Her curiosity is piqued.

It's almost 1 a.m., prime time to be a waitress in a bar. It isn't unusual for her to work doubles on Fridays and Saturdays, like today. She hesitates a moment longer, just as she begins to turn back to the crowded bar, she catches a glimpse of a familiar looking vehicle following the ambulance.

She leans closer to the window, trying to block the glare and, sure enough, she is able to see her uncle Don's minivan hauling tail not too far behind the swirling lights.

Her heart skips in her chest. Grandpa? Dad? Grandma?

Her dad is on the road and wouldn't be home for a couple more days.

Something is wrong. She can feel it.

She hurries back to the bar and puts the tray down. She grabs her purse from the cubby under the bar and dials her dad's cell phone. No answer. She dials Uncle Don. No answer. Next, she tries Gabby. Straight to voicemail. She doesn't want to call her grandparents and wake them up... but if something is going on, they would know. She dials their home number, no answer. Suddenly Randy has an overwhelming feeling of helplessness. Something is going on. She can feel it in her gut.

"Frank, I gotta go." She yells over the music.

The bar is packed, orders backed up.

"What's wrong?" Frank is popping the caps off two bottles of beer for a couple of pretty girls sitting at the end of the bar.

"I dunno." She distractedly types her number in the small computer to clock out.

"Hurry back if you can," he says. She detects a hint of annoyance but ignores it.

She digs through her purse, fishing out her keys as she pushes the door open with her rear-end.

She runs to her car and tosses her purse on top of the sweatshirt left by the previous occupant of that seat.

She fires up the engine and pulls onto Central, speeding off in the same direction her uncle had been heading. Her mind races with the possibilities of what could be wrong but her heart clinches thinking about it, so she shifts gears, she distracts herself. The sweatshirt next to her is filling her car with the smell of Axe body spray and she tries to remember the name of the guy who left here.

Mario? Manuel? She isn't great with names. He was a trucker passing through town who stopped at Franks for dinner; Randy offered to show him around the riveting town of Ruthshire after the bar closed. (Like mother, like daughter.) He had taken her up on it, and then he'd taken off early the next day.

She gets to the hospital, sees the minivan parked in front of the emergency room doors, and swings her beat-up 1996 Sunfire in the first row of empty parking spots.

She grabs her purse and opens the door. When she's greeted by a chilling gust of wind, she grabs the sweatshirt also. She rushes into the same large lobby her aunt and uncle had burst into moments ago. The receptionist is wearing the same neutral expression.

"Someone was just brought in, where did they go?"

"Do you have a name?" The receptionist asks flatly. Randy went with the response that would have the best odds.

"Last name Markson."

"She's in the ER now." Was all she got as a response.

She had seen two people in the van, most likely Uncle Don and Aunt Sara. By process of elimination, grandma was the patient.

"Can I see her?" Randy asks, feeling the panic starting to rise again.

"No. I'm sorry, you have to wait out here." And she nodded her head towards the large lobby waiting area.

"Where are my aunt and uncle? They just came in." She demands.

"I'm not sure. Have a seat in the waiting room and I'll see what I can find out." But the receptionist's eyes don't lift from her screen and she doesn't move to get out of her chair.

Randy sensed that too many years of dealing with endless tragedies has hardened her heart. She gathers her purse and over-sized sweatshirt from the counter and slowly walks to the middle of the large waiting room. She slips on the sweatshirt and buries her head in her hands. She inhales deeply, trying to organize her thoughts, but is overcome with the smell of the body spray that seems to be ingrained in the fabric. It's overpowering. Randy tilts her chin up to get fresh air and her eyes glisten with tears.

She's lonely.

She's scared.

She fishes her phone out of her purse and scrolls through the contacts.

So many numbers, yet no one she could/would call.

She wraps her arms around her shoulders, feeling more alone than ever before.

She has no one.

No one to just come sit with her.

No one really knows her... no one cares.

She thinks about growing up, how Grandma took care of her even though she had been such a troublemaker.

She tries her dad's phone again. Again, it goes straight to voicemail.

She tries Gabby's cell again. Again, it goes straight to voicemail.

She wonders if Gabby is with her parents.

She wonders what happened to grandma.

She wonders where her dad is.

She wonders if this void in her chest will ever go away.

It felt like days, but less than an hour later, she hears footsteps running towards her.

She looks up expecting to see a nurse, but instead she sees her uncle Don sprinting to the exit door. His eyes are not looking anywhere except straight ahead. Randy calls out to him as he is almost out the door. Startled at the sound of his name, he turns around, confused.

After a split second he registers who is calling him and he rushes over to embrace her.

Randy feels like he's hugging her with every fiber of his being. She starts to cry. After a full minute, she pulls back to look at his face.

He talks first, "What are you doing here?"

"I saw you following the ambulance and figured something was wrong."

Then she asked the million-dollar question, "What happened?"

"We're not sure... it looks like she rolled her car."

Randy's face twists in confusion, her eyebrows furrow, "What?!?! Where was she?"

"Um, well, we think Rick's house."

The light bulb clicks and Randy is overcome with a whole new wave of emotions.

She sinks into the chair as she realizes he's talking about Gabby.

"Is she going to be alright?"

When her uncle doesn't reply, she looks up to see tears running down his cheeks. He tries to talk but all he can muster is a shrug. His face contorts as he visibly tries to control his emotions. Randy stands up and they embrace for another long, silent moment.

"Your Aunt Sara is in the waiting room at the end of the hall on the left. She'd really appreciate your company." Then Don gives her a final squeeze and turns to hurry out the door.

Randy watches the automatic doors close behind him and once again, she's left alone.

Her thoughts bombard her. Her heart bursts. She would trade anything in the world for someone to talk to right now.

She has no one. Just a forgotten, over-scented sweatshirt.

Gabby is probably her closest friend, and they're not even that close. Randy knows Aunt Sara needs comforting, a shoulder to cry on but Randy can't even get her own thoughts in order, much less be helpful to anyone else. She doesn't think she can be strong for her aunt right now, but she slowly walks down the hall. She pauses for a moment before opening the door and then steps timidly inside.

Sara smiles faintly when she sees her. The two embrace as Sara briefly explains what happened.

Randy asks, "How can I help? What can I do?" Her large blue eyes are pleading for a task, some way to help.

"Could you call Caroline, Jude, and Nick? Just let them know what's going on."

Randy nods and pulls out her phone.

She dials Caroline first, steps into the corner, and lowers her voice to a whisper as a solemn face nurse enters the room.

CHAPTER 26

Don emerges from the hospital and the van is right where he left it. He slumps into the driver's seat and allows himself to go into autopilot... buckling the seatbelt, turning on the headlights, leaving his mind blank instead of allowing it to wander.

Everything feels surreal.

He glances at the dashboard clock; the green numbers tell him it is 2:08 a.m.

Is it possible that just two hours ago everything was fine? Only two hours ago he was asleep and his family was safe.

But now his life seems to be imploding.

He drives the empty streets towards their home.

He looks at all the houses, with the residents inside peacefully sleeping, blissfully unaware that his world is upside down.

His Baby Girl.

His Gabbs. The image of her on the road, covered in blood, collapsed in her mother's arms, is seared in his brain.

As he drives, every corner seems to hold a memory.

He passes the dead-end road where he taught Gabby to ride a bike.

He slows to a stop in front of the stop sign where Gabby hung a poster advertising her lemonade stand one summer, her book sale the next, and her lawn-mowing business the next.

She has always been a hard worker, yet he still pushed her even harder.

She also has an eye for business and a knack for entrepreneurship. She likes to make money, but she is far from selfish. She saves her money but also pours it out generously. One small example, brought to mind just this past week, was the May Day flower tradition that a nine-year-old Gabby had started when DJ was in kindergarten. Every year the school sold May Day flowers for $1 each, then at the end of the day on May 1st, the teachers pass them out in front of the entire class. Gabby was in second grade and hadn't received a flower yet, but she listened hopefully each year and was slightly disappointed when her name was never called. She didn't want her brother to have the same feeling, so for two weeks at the end of April that year, she looked for spare change and offered to do extra chores.

She scraped together two dollars.

She bought DJ two flowers. One from her, one from a 'friend'.

He was elated when he came home that day, proudly waving around his prizes.

Gabby hasn't missed a year since. Both boys receive May Day flowers, always purchased with her own money, and she always gives them one from her and one anonymously.

Don pulls into the driveway but can't bring himself to go in the house.

What will he say to them? His kids are close. Really close. Even though they fight, her brothers idolize her, and Gabby is extremely protective of them.

He doesn't know all the details (and he doesn't want to) but a couple years ago, DJ was having problems with one of the older boys who lives in their neighborhood. DJ came home upset about it a few times but then one day he came home crying, and with a black eye. That was the last time Don heard anything about it. A few days after that, when he asked DJ if things were better, DJ smiled and simply replied, "Yep. All taken care of."

Don was against fighting, he had done enough of it in his day to know that it didn't solve problems. Plus, in his position as a minister, he teaches (and believes) that we are to love others, and bless those who persecute you. If someone steals your coat, offer them your shirt. With that being said, he was glad his daughter had 'taken care of it'.

Yes, she was their protector... but Gabby also takes care of her brothers in other ways. As much as he wanted to give his family the world, Don's hard-earned dollars only stretch so far. Last August, right before it was time for back-to-school shopping, their minivan had worn through the brake pads. Upon further inspection, the brakes needed to be completely replaced.

There was no way the Markson's could afford that but luckily John Troug allowed him to put a fraction of the price down and work out a payment plan for the rest. (One of the benefits of living in a small town and having a solid reputation.) But the down payment had been the couple hundred dollars they had saved to buy each of the kids new shoes and one new outfit for the school year. Don and Sara talked about it that night, deciding the best way to break it to the kids.

The next morning when Don woke up to do his bible study before his run with Gabby, he found an envelope tucked into the 23rd Psalm.

A short note, written in Gabby's handwriting, simply said; "The Lord is my shepherd, I shall not want. He makes me lie down in green pastures. Hopefully this small token of appreciation will allow you to rest a little easier. Thank you for all you do."

It was wrapped around three crisp, $100 bills.

He was astounded at his daughter's heart. Her kindness and generosity never cease to amaze him.

Now she was lying in a hospital room. Her head cut open and her body shredded. What had the doctor said? If, IF? If she survived?

Don needs to get back to the hospital. For Gabby and for Sara.

As he opens the door, his phone vibrates.

Sara texted him two words. "She's gone."

His blood runs cold.

He's paralyzed.

Then it vibrates again with another text, "I'm sorry. I meant done. She's done with MRI. Now to surgery."

CHAPTER 27

Caroline looks around the small hospital waiting room that was so empty a few hours ago but is now crowded with people. She is surrounded by concerned faces.

Randy Markson is sitting next Sara. Gabby's dad is pacing the small room in unison with Jude. They are in sync, but opposite. They remind Caroline of the carnival game where the toy soldiers are marching back and forth, then spin back the opposite direction after getting shot. She and Gabby had taken the boys, DJ and Seth, to the state fair last summer and even though they boys were almost teenagers, they had played that game for almost an hour.

She glances over to see DJ on the other side of Sara. His head is in his hands, leaning over into his own lap. He looks broken, like everyone else who is jammed into this tiny, sterile space.

Seth is sitting next to Caroline. He is stoic. The kid has always been so mature for his age. He's only eleven, yet there's a calm about him.

She loves these boys, Don, and Sara. The whole family has always treated her as if she were one of their own, like her parents do with Gabby.

What will they do if Gabby doesn't make it?

What will she do if Gabby doesn't make it?

It has been hours since they have heard from a doctor.

Caroline fights away the pit in her stomach and returns to her prayers.

Leaning forward, elbows on her knees, hands folded, chin resting on her thumbs, Caroline slowly rocks back and forth and she begs God to save Gabby. She knows Evelyn and numerous others are doing the same. When her phone had rung in the middle of the night, it had woken up her parents too.

Caroline groggily answered as Evelyn and Mike peered worriedly through her doorway. Randy had had to repeat herself three times before the words registered in Caroline's cloudy brain.

Gabby was in a car accident.

She is in the hospital.

Caroline called Russel while Evelyn drove her to the hospital. Evelyn, sensing the waiting room would be full, dropped Caroline off and rushed home to start a prayer chain. She assumed the waiting room would be filled with Gabby's loved ones and she had been right.

Gabby has been in surgery almost five hours.

Everyone has paced and shifted but, for the most part, has stayed like they are now.

Caroline looks over at Randy. Her red hair is a mess, her thick eye makeup has smeared, giving her a ghoulish appearance.

Randy is more reserved than Caroline has ever seen her. They talked briefly by the vending machines. Randy had gotten a Diet Coke and Caroline was deciding between a Snickers bar and a bag of pretzels when Randy asked, "Who was the first person you called?"

Caroline decided on the pretzels, looked curiously at Randy, and answered, "Russel, but only because my parents were there, otherwise it probably would have been them."

Randy seemed to mull this over for a second, then continued, "If it had been Russel in the accident, who would you have called?"

Caroline opened the bag, leaned against the vending machine, and said, "Probably Gabby."

Caroline found the questions odd but everyone reacted differently in these situations.

Randy was scared for her cousin but there was something more... Caroline couldn't quite put her finger on it. Randy seemed to be searching for something. Caroline made a mental note to ask Gabby if anything was going on with Randy and a fresh wave of dread sweeps over her as she remembers why she's here.

She returns to her prayers. Pleading, begging, and bartering with God.

Suddenly, everyone inhales sharply as they see the door at the end of the hall swing open, and a doctor walks their way. Everyone stands up but Don and Sara rush to the doorway expectantly.

It's a different doctor than before, this one has concern etched on his face.

He starts with, "I'm Dr. Hasson. I'm a surgeon on-call here from Sioux Falls... Gabby's out of surgery." When he pauses, Caroline feels like her heart will beat out of her chest while she, along with everyone else in the room, holds her breath and waits for him to finish the sentence.

"She's stable."

The room lets out a collective sigh.

"She lost a lot of blood," he continues hesitantly, "But we were able to get her blood pressure back up..." Again, he pauses. Again, the anticipation in the room builds. "I don't know how to say it, other than this... the swelling around her brain is completely gone. The contusion under her eye missed damaging her vision by millimeters, and the cut on her leg, as deep as it was, managed to miss the artery. Any one of those having a slightly different outcome would have drastically worsened her condition and may have been fatal.

"The fact that she is stable right now is nothing short of a miracle. We're moving her to recovery but she can't have visitors until morning, and even then, it's hard to say when she'll wake up." He scans the packed room. "And it would be best if she only had a few at a time. It's a good idea for you to head home, get some rest, and come back later this afternoon." He looks expectantly around the room but when no one makes a move to leave, he gives them a 'suit yourself' nod, and pulls the door closed behind him.

No one speaks for several minutes.

Finally, Don breaks the silence.

"Thank You," he whispers. "Thank You God."

Everyone had been thinking the same thing.

Then he addressed the room, "The doctor is right. We are so thankful you all are here, but we'll be of more use to Gabby if we're rested when she wakes up. Sara and I will stay but you guys should head home. We will call as soon as she wakes up. In the meantime, please continue the prayers for healing and of thankfulness. God is good." His posture and authority have been restored, but as he finishes, his smile conveys the lingering reservations.

Respecting his wishes, one by one the family starts to file out. Hugging and offering words of encouragement as they leave. Don's parents are first, then Randy, and then Russell. But Caroline hesitates next to Jude while Russel talks to the Marksons.

"I think I should stay," she whispers.

Jude puts his arm around her and gives her a side hug, "I promise I'll call you first when anything changes. Right away."

"You're staying?"

"Yeah, for a bit. I can sleep anywhere. You need rest, you look exhausted. You need to do something about those raccoon eyes or you'll scare her when she wakes up." He winks and squeezes her shoulder reassuringly.

Caroline takes a deep breath and slowly takes the few steps to embrace Sara.

Jude is right. She's exhausted. A nap and a shower will do wonders.

She pulls back from Sara and says, "I'll be back in a few hours."

"Yes, get some rest. Oh, but can you please drop the boys off at the house?" Sara asks.

"Of cour-" Caroline starts to respond but she is cut off.

"I'm not going anywhere." The normally docile DJ has no qualms about it.

"Yeah, me either." Seth adds.

Sara looks at the boys, then back at Caroline. Her eyes are bloodshot, her face looks sunken. Sara uses what feels like the last bit of energy she has to offer Caroline a half smile.

"I'm not about to fight with them." Is all she says.

With that, Caroline and Russel leave. The boys each lay back in their stiff chairs.

Sara and Don sit by each other, Sara resting her head on his shoulder, Don resting his head on Sara's. Jude goes to the far corner and he calls Marshall. Flu or no flu he'll have to open the shop tomorrow. He can take his pretty little girlfriend in to run the desk while he stays in the can if he needs to.

Missing a day in the field is one thing. But suddenly being right here is the most important thing.

Everyone settles in and does their best to relax as they wait for the okay to migrate to Gabby's room.

CHAPTER 28

May 5, 2002

Once again I'm woken up by a bright light. This time I'm in a hospital room instead of on the side of the road. The sun is beating through the blinds into the small room, which is made even smaller by the over-sized-bed and the four other people crowded inside.

I'm lying on a typical hospital bed and there are four chairs jammed into this room that's barely bigger than a closet. The back part of the bed is elevated so I'm halfway laying down, halfway sitting up.

I look down and see DJ laying next to me, all 6 feet of him. His head is resting on my left arm, his legs curled up next to mine, and the middle half his body is hanging off the bed.

Seth is sprawled out in a chair in the corner, his head hanging over the back.

A small blanket is hanging from his lap, mostly on the floor. There is an empty chair beside him.

Mom and Dad are each contorted into, what appear to be, the most uncomfortable positions imaginable. They are sitting in cushioned folding chairs along the wall close to the bed.

My family.

It takes a second to make sense of it all, but it quickly comes back to me. All the pieces snap into place.

The phone call, the ambulance ride, the doctors.

But it's kinda fuzzy. None of it's very clear.

My arms and legs are bandaged. Not like the exaggerated comics where they're completely wrapped like mummies and they have their extremities hanging from support poles. No, my right leg is covered in gauze and wrapped in a beige bandage. My left leg is wrapped in something stronger than a bandage but not quite a cast. My arms are both covered with the gauze from elbow to wrist.

I gingerly lift my hand to feel my face.

I have a wave of relief wash over me when my fingers brush against soft skin, my mind flashing back to the scaly sensation from before.

There is a dull ache in my head but the shooting knife pains are gone.

I slowly move my fingers across my cheeks, my nose, and my mouth. Everything seems to be in order. I can feel a bandage under my left eye... then I graze my hand over my forehead. The knife pains shoot through and cause me to breathe in sharply. The bandage starts right above my eyebrows, wraps on top of my ears, and covers the whole top of my head.

I don't feel any hair. Am I bald?

Guess I won't have to worry about my frizzy hair at prom.

I try to swallow but my mouth feels like I have cotton balls shoved from my teeth clear back to my tonsils.

There is an overwhelming smell of iron engulfing me. It's enough to make me gag. As I open my mouth and hack, Jude walks in, sullenly carrying a cup coffee. He glances at the bed, and when he sees my eyes are open, his face brightens.

"Hey," he whispers, breaking out in a smile as he makes his way over to the bedside, stepping over sprawled feet, and miscellaneous items scattered on the floor.

"Wh-at?" My voice cracks. My lips are dry. I'm so thirsty.

"It's ok, it's ok. Don't try to talk." Jude rests his hand on top of mine and squeezes tenderly.

My dad hears the conversation and sits up quickly, dropping his phone on the floor, which startles my mom. Neither one need any time to find their bearings, they each rush to over me. Jude steps out of the way so my parents can be on both sides of the bed, each grabbing one of my hands.

My mom lightly brushes my hair back and kisses my cheek. It hurts but I try not to flinch.

DJ stirs and groggily opens his eyes. When he sees what's going on, he eagerly sits up. He shifts to the foot of the small bed so he's facing me and a smile pulls at his lips.

"Bout time." he teases. Mom ignores him and takes my face lightly in both her hands.

I can tell she wants to say something but she's not being able to. I search my mom's tear-filled, bloodshot eyes. I see relief and love.

I turn to my dad. Tears are streaming his cheeks and his face is clinched up, he's trying so hard not to cry.

I try again to ask what's going on but, "Whaa-" is all that comes out.

176

I look questioningly at my parents. When they still reveal nothing, I turn my attention back to Jude who is leaning against the doorway. He's letting our family have a moment but he smiles, nods, and says, "It was close. Looks like you were auditioning for Nascar or somethin'. You're a pretty lucky kid. God is good."

CHAPTER 29

May 18, 2002

The flowers, cards, and stuffed animals that filled my hospital room now clutter up my bedroom. The doctors kept me in the hospital for a week to keep an eye on me. The fact that they couldn't explain my drastic improvement concerned them.

It's been thirteen days since the accident, and I feel good.

I'm still sore, still have the dull ache in my head, but possibly the most peculiar side-effect is the still-present scent of blood.

It's nauseating.

I have showered multiple times, but with my gaping head wound still healing and partially open, the smell (and taste) of dried blood seems to be my new aroma.

On the bright side, the smell is largely due to the blood that soaked into my hair which means they didn't end up shaving my head. I'm not bald, it was just all bandaged.

Even though I didn't show signs of significant repercussions, the doctor strongly recommended at least one more full week of bed rest.

So here I sit; on the last day of the mandatory sentence, in my room, surrounded by gifts, watching Friends on TV, and scribbling in my journal, when there is a knock on the door.

I look up from my notebook as Randy opens the door and saunters in. Not surprisingly, Jude and Caroline have visited every day while I was in the hospital and after I was moved home.

What was unexpected is that my cousin has also not missed a day of dropping by to chat.

"How's the prisoner? Ummmm, I mean patient?" Randy winks and offers a sideways grin, shuffling a few pieces of paper out of the way, clearing a place for her to sit on the bed next to me.

She can't help it. Seduction radiates off her even when she's not trying. Years of practice have made flirting Randy's main form of communication. Even in regular conversations. I feign annoyance but smile at her. The past couple weeks we have become closer than ever.

Our conversations have gone past the superficial 'How's the weather?' and catching up on family gossip. We have discussed, at length, topics that we never breached before. Morals, dreams, church, and God, just to name a few. I have noticed a subtle and gradual change in my wildly confident cousin.

I can't pinpoint it, but it is as if Randy is searching for something, and she thinks I know where it is.

"How are ya feeling?" Randy looks at me with genuine concern.

"Fine... well... better. Yeah, my head hurts and I'm exhausted but I think that's partly because I'm trapped in this bed. But tomorrow I'll be able to get up and around. That'll be nice."

"Yeah, it's hard to believe it's already been two weeks since the accident but it's also hard to believe it's only been two weeks, ya know?"

I smile and laugh because I do know. I feel exactly the same way.

I subconsciously, and very carefully, touch the wound on my head. Even after two weeks, it's still open and it bleeds occasionally.

Randy plays with a loose string on the bedspread as she continues, "So, I've been thinkin, about, maybe, quitting the bar."

I have to make myself close my mouth that dropped open. "Seriously? Why?"

"I need something different. I need a change." Randy pauses, takes a deep breath, and turns her stormy blue eyes to meet mine. "You can't tell anyone, but all that attention isn't good for my ego," she chuckles to show she's kidding but I can tell there's truth to the statement.

She continues, "I have a crazy idea that I'm working on... It may take a few months, but I think it'll be great. I'll need your help."

Before I have a chance to respond, there's another knock on the door and Erik pops his dreadlocks-covered head in.

"Another jam-packed night of sitting around I see..." he begins his ridicule while still opening the door, midway through his sentence, he notices Randy and quickly backtracks, "Oh I'm sorry, I didn't mean to interrupt."

He has stopped in before every shift to give me a hard time about not coming to work. Melinda, a soft-spoken and reserved bookworm has filled in to cover most of my shifts and Erik isn't happy about it.

"No worries," Randy hooks a grin on the corner of her mouth, slightly biting her bottom lip, and makes a production of rolling off the bed before raising her arms above her head and stretching suggestively.

And just like that, Randy is back to her old self, back in all her Randy glory, as she presses against him on her way out the door.

"I was just leaving. We'll talk soon Gabbs." She shoots that patented Randy wink as she saunters out the door.

Erik watches her walk down the hallway and leans back to catch the last glimpse of her heading up the stairs. I roll my eyes. "Whenever you're done gawking, I have a few new jokes about your mama driving you around."

Erik comes into the room, moves a giant vase of tulips from one of the chairs onto the floor, and sits down across from me.

"Get 'um in while you can. Only a few more months..." The statement is directed at me but it also sounds like he's reminding himself. Then, with a chuckle, he tacks on, "I'll be driving before you will."

He shoots me an antagonistic grin and crosses one leg over his knee. "So, Gabbs, in all honesty, this accident... your head getting messed up, your car totaled, your arms and legs all cut up, how do you factor that in with your God? Still believe in Him? Still think he's good?"

He's hinted about the subject before but never asked outright.

I didn't hesitate for a second with my response, "I've never believed more."

And I proceed to tell him the laundry list of reasons why that is true.

CHAPTER 30

August 2002

My eyes are straight ahead.

The sweat from my brow burns as it drips in my eyes, my face is damp from perspiration.

I'm focused on my breathing. Deep breath in, then empty my lungs.

I inhale through my nose, then push all the air out through my mouth.

I breathe in again, so deeply it feels like my lungs will burst.

I imagine the fresh oxygen flowing through my body, giving new energy to my aching legs.

Then I push all the air out, visualizing eliminating all the toxins from my body.

I am seated on a weight bench.

I straighten my legs, pushing the weighted bar up.

The bar clicks against the metal, and I lower it back down.

My running has been replaced by physical therapy.

The leg press is the last activity for today.

The recovery has been a slow process, contradicting how speedily I seemed to initially bounce back. Getting back to my old self has been a challenge.

What the medical professionals thought was soreness from the impact, turned out to be a dislocated vertebra in my neck. I also popped a shoulder out of its socket and, while it missed an artery in my leg, the glass did cut the muscle. It has healed substantially but has resulted in a slightly noticeable limp. The physical therapy process is painful but I can see and feel the progress.

Twice a week, every week, I've been here building up strength and stretching out muscles.

The accident caused a lot of damage to my body that will affect me to some degree the rest of my life.

But thanks to Nicole, my physical therapist, the effects should be minimal.

The mental exercises are not as measurable but twice as frustrating.

I was diagnosed with TBI (Traumatic Brain Injury) about a month after I was released from the hospital. When the after-effects didn't go away as they should, the doctors ran more tests and concluded TBI was the culprit. The main symptoms I suffer from are forgetfulness, seizures, and headaches. Another constant reminder of that night is the scar that covers a majority of my forehead. The doctor has recommended a plastic surgeon, but I think I'm just gonna make the look work. The jagged, raised scar is very noticeable. Mostly because it was a patch job. The nurses combed through my hair, rinsing the blood and ripped pieces of scalp out, and then they pieced it back together as best they could. The hair around the scar on my head is finally starting to grow in but I suspect it will always be noticeable, and that's ok.

I should be gearing up to finish my college degree and taking advantage of all the credits I got for participating in the high school placement program. Instead, I will be retaking two of the courses I failed last year due to missing the final.

My dreams of being a vet are on hold, at best. And I keep telling myself that that's ok, too.

What matters is that I have my friends, my family, and my faith.

There are lots of rumors about what had happened that night. The most popular one is that I got drunk and simply lost control.

The truth doesn't matter to those people who spread the lies or the people who believe them.

They weren't interested in what really happened, although I think the irony itself would be enough to sway them to the truth... it was even in the official police report.

The officer who had been so intent on finding proof that I had been drinking and driving, well he stumbled on the actual cause of the accident.

A cow.

I'm not even kidding.

Dad and Jude met the police at the scene the next day, in the light, and the evidence of what happened was clear; I had been driving down the middle of the gravel road, when I topped the hill (going faster than I should have been, I was runnin late, remember?) I swerved to miss a cow that had gotten out of its fence and wandered to the road.

I slammed on the brake, but my foot must have slipped to the gas pedal because I accelerated into the ditch. They could tell I scared the cow because there was physical evidence of exactly where it been standing, and the tires left imprints in the gravel of where I veered off the road.

The series of events were easily explained but what was difficult to give an account for was how I came out as well as I did.

The number of variables that worked together that night for my survival are innumerable.

*The temp being colder than normal, which slowed down the blood loss.

*Nick calling exactly when he did, bringing me back to consciousness.

*My seatbelt not staying fastened. Had I been strapped in upside down, I would have bled to death.

*Dr. Hasson, the surgeon, happened to be in town and able to fill in for the regular on-call doctor who had next-to-no surgical experience and was ill.

*My cellphone should not have worked at all. The amount of initial damage and blood that crept into it should have shorted it out immediately, but it functioned long enough for Dad to calm me down and for them to find me.

I could go on and on.

There is no explanation, other than divine intervention.

God saved me.

I push the weighted bar up, "Fifteen!" and releases it.

My last set.

I collapse back on the bench for a break.

"You got 5 minutes, then we're stretching." Nicole hands me a water bottle and walks away.

I use the break to check my phone.

Caroline texted 'Finished my application. Yours done yet?'

I have noticed that most people treat me differently now.

I'm not sure if it is the scar, the limp, or the story but I'm definitely not 'Girl in Hallway' anymore.

I'm 'Girl who almost died and now has an oozing head wound'.

Turns out 'Girl in Hallway' wasn't that bad.

Lots of people stare. Lots of people look at me with pity. Lots of people give me special treatment.

But not Caroline.

She expects me to give my best, no excuses.

She doesn't accept the doctor's recommendation for me to postpone college due to the memory issues. Caroline is set on sticking to our original plan even though I know it is highly unlikely with my injuries, I appreciate her pushing me. She has been a great friend through the whole event. So has Jude. So has Randy. Even Nick helps out and checks up on me often.

One person I haven't talked to since the accident is Rick. I have seen him out and about, but we've never talked. He didn't come to visit in the hospital or even when I was moved home. He never bothered to break up with me but with my strong powers of deductive reasoning, I figured that not speaking for three months probably meant we were over.

Even with all that; the accident, the totaled car, the gashed in head, TBI, the unsure future, and getting dumped, I can't help but smile.

One thing about nearly dying is that your perspective changes and your priorities realign.

I realized I wasted so much time the past year wrestling with the two images of myself and trying to figure out which one I wanted to be that I was missing out on so much that was happening right now.

But, leaving the hospital a week after almost dying, I have a clarity most adults are still searching for.

I give a lot of credit to the lovely counselor, Dr. Bremher, who went beyond the therapy needed for trauma caused by the accident and, for the first time in my life, helped me to see that how I had been dealing with my emotions was not the norm.

She helped me talk through *the incident* and helped me identify the defense mechanisms my mind put in place. The boxing up, the walling off, the shutting down.

And she helped me see that there aren't two versions of myself. There is just one Gabby. And that is enough.

After a few months I was finally able to accept that.

Maybe it was seeing the people I love the most, love me for just being me.

After the accident I didn't have the strength to pretend or to put on a show. I hadn't been able to put up any fronts.

I just WAS.

And I have never been happier.

I'm still smiling at the thought as Nicole walks back over and I hear the familiar rumbling of Jude's truck pull up outside.

I'm still without a car of my own so my friends and parents have been taking turns shuttling me around, much to Erik's delight.

Today Jude will be driving from therapy to work.

I take one more swig of water and sit back, preparing to do my final stretches.

I no longer feel the pressure of choosing between the two Gabbys, or the stress of turning one into the other.

I now know that both 'versions' are just layers of my true self.

I had been trying to fit into a mold that wasn't made for me.

I am good, like Caroline.

I am also fun, like Randy. (Not as much fun, but still fun.)

I am also rebellious.

I love God and I know He has a plan for my life... even though I don't know what it is yet.

But for now, I'm just enjoying being Gabby.

Fun, yet responsible.

Independent, yet reliant.

Strong. yet vulnerable (Sometimes.)

Imperfect, but improving.

Just Gabby.

And I am happy with that... finally.

EPILOGUE

Well, there you have.

That's my story.

It's hard to believe that it's been five years since that all went down.

So much has happened since then.

For starters, I finally know who I am.

I am Gabby.

I am loved.

I am broken.

I am complicated.

And that's ok.

I have been told my whole life that God loves me.

I always believed it. I still do, but the thought that He spared me because he has a plan for me. Well, that was new. It gave me purpose. God will use me, Gabby, as broken as I am, for His good.

I use the hurts from my life to help others. I work at a women's shelter. I can sympathize with their stories of abuse. I also speak at high schools on the importance of self-love and not keeping secrets, at the end of each session we open up for anonymous confessions.

And I write.

I wrote my story to show women they're not alone and I write to encourage others to speak out.

The idea that Randy had that day she came down to my room was for a fresh start.

My accident was a wakeup call for her, too. She wanted more. With as confident as she appeared and with as many admires as she had, I had no idea how lonely she felt.

She also struggled with loving herself.

She finally started coming to church with us.

She started praying and letting God's love wash over her.

And she wanted a fresh start but didn't think she could do it on her own.

So, after I graduated that next year, we loaded up her red Sunfire and moved to Des Moines.

Just the two of us.

Randy enrolled right away at a community college here in town and quickly got her crime scene investigators certificate. Now she's going to school at a major university not too far from here where she's working towards her Forensic Science degree.

She's putting herself though school by working at a department store and as a police dispatcher, trying to get her foot in the door.

She works all the time and doesn't make as much as she did at the bar but I've never seen my cousin so happy.

She's driven and is passionate about dead bodies. (I don't get it, but that's her thing.)

Once she graduates, she will move to a bigger city where there are more murders and more corpses.

I won't go with her this time. I've settled in nicely here. It took me a little longer to get back into the groove of school when we moved down so I have one more year left and then I will have my counseling degree.

I hope to open my own practice here in town where I will specialize in helping young victims of abuse.

My dreams of becoming a vet were never realized and I am okay with that. Really, I am. I satisfy my need to help animals by volunteering at the humane society. Plus, Randy and I have total of three dogs and two cats cluttering up the little two-bedroom house we rent.

Missy is getting pretty gray but she's still feisty and greets me with her little wiggle whenever I come home.

Nick was such a blessing to me that night and we still keep in touch. He moved out to the west coast and is a computer whiz for some high-tech company.

Caroline might be the most surprising story of us all. The girl who was so gung-ho on us going away to the same school, well, she actually skipped college.

She had some time to reflect after my accident and she realized that life is short and that what she really loves to do is paint.

So, she moved to New York, like she wanted.

She struggled for a few years, like she wanted.

And then she caught her big break, like she wanted.

One morning she was flipping through her sketch book when she was on break at the little coffee shop where she worked, when some hot shot peered over her shoulder and saw her amazing drawings.

He asked her to draw him a cup of coffee. She whipped out her pencils and sketched a latte, complete with decorative foam, in minutes.

He offered her a job on the spot. She turned in her notice to the coffee shop that day.

She's not filthy rich, yet. But she loves her life. That hot shot commissioned her to paint murals in his home and office building he owns. She has multiple other jobs on the horizon from his big-time friends.

I am so proud of her and I hope to go visit her soon. She and Russel are still doing the long-distance thing. He's in medical school now. Yeah, gonna be a doctor married to a successful artist. I am so proud of my friends.

My family is all doing great.

DJ graduated high school and is going to college down here near me, he is still not sure what he wants to major in but he's enjoying living the college life.

Seth is still in high school. He's a good kid but a handful.

Mom and Dad are better than I can ever remember.

Dad even picked up a couple hobbies. He makes time almost every weekend to fish and he takes mom out a on a date at least once a week.

I think that pretty much catches you up with everyone. Oh yeah... except Jude.

As I type this, he has wrapped his arms around my shoulders. His scruff is tickling my neck. Just like everyone else I love, that night was a turning point for him, too.

He waited six months after the accident before he told me; but waiting in the waiting room that night, not knowing if I would wake up, he decided that he had been fooling himself.

He loved me.

I loved him too, of course.

But up to that point I had a hard enough time loving myself that I didn't recognize what it would look like to truly love someone else.

After counseling, after I healed, after he saw that I was better (like a lot better) we went for a drive.

I noticed he was acting differently, but then again, everyone had been.

He pulled over onto one of the farmers' roads on his property.

He didn't dance around it at all. "Here's the thing, kid. You know I love ya. But... I love you." And he looked at me with those green eyes and my heart opened like never before. No boxes. No walls.

It was terrifying and exhilarating.

He leaned over. Then he softly brushed a strand of slightly frizzy hair off my cheek and tucked it behind my ear. Tracing his thumb down the curve of my face he gently used two fingers under my chin to bring my mouth to his. His lips were soft. His touch was gentle.

Time stopped.

I felt loved. I felt safe.

That's what a first kiss is supposed to be.

That's the first kiss I will remember.

And I think it'll end up being my last first kiss.

We dated the rest of my senior year. When Randy asked me to move with her, I felt like it was something I had to do.

Jude was completely supportive but after a year of the long-distance thing, he found a job down here. He still goes home quite a bit to help on the farm but he's looking to buy land around here.

All in all, that night was the start of a brand-new path for me and everyone I love.

It didn't just alter my career path but it also changed how I saw myself and how I live my life.

My greatest source of hurt and shame is now what fuels me.

The accident and *the incident*, both traumatic events that threated to ruin me, have veered my life in a direction I never would have taken.

It's been a wonderful experience and I can't wait to see what's next.

Stay tuned.

Acknowledgements

You'll probably skim these (to be honest I usually do too) but the next few pages have as much honesty and love packed into them as any other. These are my people. These are my life.

My Husband: Your support and belief in me is the main reason I am able to live out my dreams. If I was half the person in reality that I am in your eyes, I would be twice the person I really am. You are a constant source of strength, not just in my endeavors, but in who I am. I love you.

My Children: You inspire me. You are my WHY in all that I do and all I aspire to be. Try as I might, I can't put into words my absolute adoration for you. Being your mom is my greatest joy. I love you more than you'll ever know.

My Mom: You've read every word I've ever written. Thank you for giving the love of reading and the passion to tell stories. Thank you for filling my childhood with a healthy balance of Disney and Columbo, which has enabled me to grow into a woman who can carry entire conversations with movie quotes while also harboring a healthy dose of suspicion at all times.
Thank you for showing me what it looks like to be a great mom.

My Dad: Thanks for passing on your faith, work ethic, and focus. Thank you for the hours spent studying God's word and the lifetime example you've been of what it looks like to have a close relationship with Him. Thank you for teaching me how to be self-sufficient but also for always being there, whether it's to escort me across Iowa in a snow storm or walking me step-by-step through relighting a pilot light in a gas furnace so I wouldn't freeze.

Bub and Z: My first friends and original fan club. I am so lucky to have you as brothers but even more thankful to have you both as friends. The inside jokes, our adventures, and even the rallying together during the tough times are some of my most treasured memories. I am immeasurably blessed by the family I was born into and I am so thankful for the love and support I have been surrounded with my entire life.

Jackie Sue: You've had blind faith that this is what I was meant to do before it was even on my radar... Without your support, reassurance, and nudging, I would have given up. Words can't express my appreciation for you and our friendship. Even after all these years I am sometimes surprised that there is another 'me' living clear across the country.
I love you Sis.

Jessi: You are my counterpart in all the ways I need you to be. You remind me who I am... but still encourage me to be better. Your optimism, perspective, and loving upfront honesty are a few of the many ways you inspire me. You are an example of strength and finding humor in the worst of circumstances. Thank you for all the weekends away and thank you for always being there. I love you.

Tiffany: You see the best in me, even when I've shown you the worst. You remind me that I am a beloved daughter of The King while also holding me accountable. You are an example to me of a Christian, wife, and mother that I want to be.
Thank you for keeping me centered.
Thank you for always offering what I need; be it comfort, support, encouragement or a gallon of ice cream. I love you.

Blair: Thank you for listening intently, week after week, about the slow process of this (and so many other) projects. Thank you for indulging me in all the *seemingly* meaningless conversations (about running, cleaning, scheduling, need for personal space, and kids) and helping to reassure me that I'm not the only one with quirks. Thanks for always being willing to eat too much, have a girls' night out, and for knowing what to say to make me laugh. Your friendship has been such a blessing. I love you.

You: If you haven't been listed yet but have read all the way through (even the acknowledgements) then I am especially thankful for you. I am thankful you bought my book and I hope you enjoyed it. I am thankful you took the time to read about these characters that I love so much and I am thankful you took the time to read through the shout-outs of the real life people who have made me who I am. YOU, you are awesome.

Finally, and most of all, my Heavenly Father.
I am in my thirties, and, at times, I still act like a rebellious teenager. Thank you for loving me unconditionally, for blessing me far beyond my worth and for continually bestowing me with unmerited (but very necessary) grace.

Made in the USA
Monee, IL
27 June 2023